# DARK THINGS

by

**Joseph F. Brown**

Josh - Hi. I hope you like my story and don't get too scared! Best wishes.
Joe
OSF
9-3-95

Royal Fireworks Press
*Unionville, New York*
*Toronto, Ontario*

Royal Fireworks Press
First Avenue
Unionville, NY 10988
(914) 726-4444
FAX: (914) 726-3824

Royal Fireworks Press
78 Biddeford Avenue
Downsview, Ontario
M3H 1K4 Canada
FAX: (416) 633-3010

ISBN: 0-88092-110-2 Paperback
0-88092-111-0 Library Binding

Printed in the United States of America on recycled acid-free paper by the Royal Fireworks Press of Unionville, New York.

CHAPTER ONE

# Jarrod

"And now, ladies and gentlemen, I present Jarrod, the Wonder Boy!" The Great Blackwell swooped his hands high into the air, his black leather cape snapping upward like the wings of some giant prehistoric bat. Two pole lanterns, one on each side of the small wooden stage, suddenly roared out tongues of orange flame. As the crowd gasped, the magician closed the cape around himself, twirled once, and then slowly opened his arms. In front of him stood his son.

"Thank you, thank you," the ten year old said, having to shout above the applause. He swept his hands high into the air, his own cape snapping upward, then skipped over to a small velvet-skirted table. On the table was an empty wooden chest. Jarrod showed the crowd how empty it was by tilting it toward them. There was more applause.

"Let there be magic," The Great Blackwell ordered, reaching out with his wand. The boy held both hands together. When the tip of the wand touched them, there was a flash of brightness—and then the hands were golden. Jarrod held them up and moved his fingers. Each sparkled in the light of the torches. The crowd gasped in amazement.

"A chest is for treasure, and this has none," the young magician explained. Slowly, he placed his hands into the open chest and began to feel the smoothness of the bottom. His eyes closed and his head tilted back as the tips of his golden fingers caressed the wood. In a few moments, he was lost in a dream deeper than all of eternity.

The dream began in darkness. There was the feel of the wood, the hush of the crowd, and the smells of oil lamps, the warm night, cigars and perfume. Jarrod thought he heard the shrill buzzing sound of a mosquito dancing around his ear, but soon that faded. There was silence. Then the speck of light appeared, far away in the distance. It drifted at first, like a single firefly above the floor of the darkest woods. The boy felt his excitement growing as the light became still.

There was a hesitation—and then the light exploded to fill the darkness. Within the light were images of all that Jarrod wanted the dream to be. They started out too small to see, and then puffed up so fast there almost wasn't enough time to see all that they showed. Before he knew it, the images and the light had blown past, and the dream was over.

Jarrod opened his eyes. His hands were still inside the open chest, only the chest was filled with gold dust. What the audience would think an amazing trick had not been a trick at all, but an inexplicable act of creation.

The boy smiled and scooped up two handfuls of the precious dust. As he let it flow back down into the chest, the crowd applauded.

"A treasure fit for a king! Or a king's son." As Jarrod continued to scoop and pour the gold dust, he changed his voice so it sounded like that of an older woman.

"Little king, come and eat your supper. The cooks have prepared your favorite—vegetables." Some in the audience laughed. Jarrod changed his voice again, to that of a small child.

"Not now, Ma-ma. Can't you see I'm playing with my gold?" There was more laughter.

In his normal voice, Jarrod asked, "But how long do you think the king's son could play with his gold, before he would become bored? Not very long, I would say. No, the king's son would want more to play with than just his gold. He'd want toys, maybe living toys, maybe living toys inspired by the dragons that lived at the far reaches of the kingdom..."

Out from the gold dust, the young magician withdrew his hands. Cupped inside of them was something that moved. There was a noise then, like a high-pitched squawk. Whatever it was began to struggle and make even more noise—and then Jarrod released it.

A miniature dragon, about the size of a robin, flapped upward into the night air. It went right over the astonished crowd, looked down, and let out a tiny shriek. Then it spotted a large moth dancing around the torch on the right side of the stage. It turned, flapped back, and swooped downward. In an instant, it had the helpless insect in its fanged jaws.

The dream creation immediately began to feed. It turned again and headed back out over the crowd. Then, it started to fade away. First the body began to evaporate and then the wings. Within a few seconds, the miniature dragon was gone. Only the partially-chewed moth remained above the spectators. It moved along for a few seconds more, then slowly arched downward, its one extended wing causing it to spiral like a seed falling from an elm tree.

The tiny remains were snatched out of the air by the plump hand of a fat man wearing fancy boots, striped pants, a dress coat, and top hat. Jarrod guessed him to be wealthy, maybe a merchant or banker. The man held up what was left of the moth and bellowed in astonished laughter. Some others laughed too, out of amazement, and most of the others clapped their hands.

The people soon turned their attention back toward the stage and were delighted by other acts of magic. The Wonder Boy was able to create any small object anyone from the audience called out. Each time, he closed his eyes, let his hands sift through the gold dust in the chest, and dreamed of what he would create. Seconds later, he pulled it out for all to see. Some of the objects had only temporary existence while others were permanent. Which it was depended upon Jarrod's whim at the moment of creation.

Near the end of the show, The Great Blackwell stepped down into the audience, picked spectators at random, and waved his magic wand above them. Moments later, his son would pull from the chest whatever had been in their pockets.

One young man was greatly embarrassed when he went up to the stage to retrieve his transported possessions. Mixed in with the watch, the small amount of money, and pouch of chewing tobacco were several poker chips. Beside him was his young wife, to whom he had sworn he had given up gambling. She slapped his face and stomped off in a great huff. Everyone—except the young man—laughed.

Soon, the show was over, and the crowd had gone home. It took the Blackwells about a half hour to put out the torches, disassemble the stage, and stow everything back into the wagon. They had sold fifty-one five-cent tickets, taking in a total of two dollars and fifty-five cents, a good sum of money for Salem, Oregon, in the year 1867.

Later, they had dinner at the Coachhouse Saloon. The Great Blackwell, whose real name was Ben, had two helpings of stew, bread, and corn on the cob. Jarrod had a single helping.

"Got corn in my teeth?" the boy asked, showing a mouthful of corn-covered teeth.

"Not as much as I do," Ben answered, showing his own. They stared at each other for a few seconds, trying to pretend to be serious—then started laughing. They didn't even notice the man named Twil Ringers come up to their table. When they did, they laughed even more.

"I'm sorry," Ben was finally able to say, motioning with his hand for Twil to wait while he swished his mouth with water. After swallowing, he continued, "Again, my apologies. Thank you for waiting. How may I help you?"

"Well I guess you two sure do have fun. That's what I heard, you know, though I ain't never seen you before. It's good for a man and his boy to laugh and joke, yes sir. No need to apologize, no sir. Mr. Blackwell, Boy, my name is Twil Ringers, and I have a message from Mr. Clement. Ah, he's my boss out at Opal Creek Mine. Fine man, Mr. Clement." The older man paused, then held out a small brown envelope. "A message for you from Mr. Clement."

"Thank you," Ben said, taking the envelope.

"Thank you. Ah, good night now. Night, Boy." Twil excused himself with a slight bowing gesture and left.

Jarrod took a sip of water and swished his own mouth clean as his father opened the envelope.

"It's an invitation. This Mr. Clement is wondering if we'd come to his mine and do a show for his family and crew. It's his son's tenth birthday."

"Sounds good to me," Jarrod said. "Where's Opal Creek Mine?"

"East of here. Here's the map. He's even offering to pay fifteen dollars." As Ben laid the small map on the table, the two exchanged a private look. People thought the gold dust was fake, and all the magic was some kind of illusion, but the truth was, Jarrod could create as much real gold as he wanted. They sold tickets and collected small amounts of money, but only so no one would think they were rich and try to rob them.

The two finished their meal, left fifty cents on the table, and started to leave. The Coachhouse was crowded, smoky, and noisy. Most of the customers were men. Those at the tables were playing cards and drinking while those at the bar were just drinking. Jarrod loved the excitement of crowded places. All the sounds seemed to talk directly to him. Squeaking floor boards, the banging piano, the laughing and shouting people—even the spittoons seemed to be aimed directly at his ears. The sounds came jumbled together, but he heard each one in all its richness.

Smells came directly too. In one deep breath, the boy could imagine the recent history of the place. It was as if he had been there all day, walking around all over, watching people come and go. "Do me a trick," the bartender said, startling Jarrod out of his sensing. "You're the Wonder Boy, aren't you?"

"I am."

"You should've stayed dressed in your capes and top hats. Been good for business."

"But maybe not so good for enjoying a quiet meal—which was very good, by the way."

The bartender nodded his acceptance of the compliment, finished wiping a glass, and leaned over the bar, closer to the young magician.

"Okay, but let's make it interesting." Son looked at father, and the wink of an eye gave permission to have some fun. Jarrod stepped up to the bar and leaned over on it, nearly coming face to face with the very large man.

"If I can read your mind and tell you things that happened in here today, dinner is on the house. If not, I pay you double." The two shook hands. Men seated on either side of the boy waved to friends, and soon there was a small crowd gathered around.

"Okay," Jarrod started, taking a long deep breath and closing his eyes. Dozens of smells, some so faint they barely existed, ballooned into images. He opened his eyes, looked deeply into those of the bartender, and continued, "You ran out of your regular lye soap and had to use…a lady's bath soap to mop the floors this morning." The big man leaned back, surprised, but said nothing.

"You had someone in to unclog the drain in the bathroom urinal... It's okay now. A woman..." The magician paused to look around at those who had gathered in close. Another sniff, and he pointed. "That woman hugged you or was close to you about three o'clock this afternoon..." The woman let out a gasping laugh and covered her mouth to stifle more. Everyone else became quiet.

"A group of cowboys was in. They were sheep herders."

"Then they ain't no cowboys," someone interrupted before being hushed by the others.

"About six of them. Their boots weren't very clean. You got new ice today for your cooler...ah, something spilled in the back. Pickles, yeah, the pickle barrel was leaking. And..." Jarrod paused and looked even deeper into the amazed man's slightly bulging eyes. "Another woman. You..."

"That's wonderful!" the bartender blurted out. In a move so quick it could have been made by a magician, he reached into his pocket, withdrew a fifty-cent piece, and slapped it down on the counter.

"Who's he talking about, hun?" the woman who had stifled her laugh asked.

"No one, doll, no one at all. Just pretend, that's all." The others started laughing.

"Thanks," Jarrod said, collecting the coin.

"These too," the bartender offered. He reached over and handed Jarrod five quarter-sized tokens. "You come back."

"Thank you, we will," Ben smiled. "Good night, ladies, gentlemen. Son."

As the two walked out toward the swinging doors, those inside the saloon began to applaud. Jarrod waved once, then followed his father outside.

"Neat, Dad, look. Ah, what's a 'Quiet Smile'? Each of these is good for one."

"Quiet Smile's one-tenth of a pint of whiskey in its own little bottle. The Crystal Palace in Tombstone, Arizona, has ones just like it. You better hang on to them for a few years." The ten-year-old looked at them some more, then tucked them away in his front pants pocket. The two continued down the wooden sidewalk, toward their wagon.

"How'd you know he'd been with two women? Most of 'em wear the same perfume."

"Especially in saloons." Jarrod fanned his hand in front of his face, exaggerating. "Ah, I didn't. It was a guess. A man like that, I just figured. I ran out of things I could tell him from the smells, and I wasn't sure if it was good enough to win, so I figured I'd say something that would make him stop me." The two laughed.

CHAPTER TWO

# The Road East

It was close to midnight when The Great Blackwell and his son, The Wonder Boy, left Salem. Their strong and trusting horse, Ferdinand, slowly pulled them along. Ferdi, as they called him, was used to midnight work. His masters liked to play with other forms of magic—forms that could never be played with around other people. Soon, they connected with the Santiam Trail and headed east, toward Opal Creek Mine.

The moon was bright and the night warm, perfect for imagining. The first contest was to spot a popcorn tree. This could be any tree, but would probably be a blue spruce in some small clearing, probably up on a hillside. In the moonlight, it would look almost gray and almost blue at the same time. All a person had to do was stop and imagine it covered with popcorn, and it would seem to turn almost yellow. The blue and gray were so close to faint yellow that the mere suggestion would trick the mind into seeing what was not there.

"There's one!" Jarrod called out, being the first one to spot a likely candidate.

"Ferdi, whoa," Ben said. Horse and wagon soon stopped, and the two stared up at the tree. A few moments later, Ben saw it change color, as if it were suddenly covered in popcorn.

"You got it."

"I see it now too! Look at all that popcorn." A few seconds later, Jarrod continued, "We can camp here. That rise, by the tree, would be good for catching."

"I don't know. I'm kind of bushed tonight. Been a long day."

"Oh, please, Dad. I feel really strong tonight. They'll be big ones, really big ones."

"You know, someday, if we're not careful, one of those big ones is going to eat us and old Ferdinand all up. Won't find a thing but our chewed-up bones."

"Just have to be careful. Please?"

After a long pause, Ben sighed, "Okay. But just one run."

It took all of thirty minutes to make camp for the night. Jarrod, bristling with extra energy, nearly flew through the routine. He started by taking off Ferdinand's reins, harness, and collar. Then he tied a long rope between two trees, attached the horse, and brushed it down. Last, he put out its food and fetched it water from a nearby creek. By then, Ben was just getting the camp fire going. Jarrod dug the latrine hole, and they were done.

"You worked hard today, Son. You earned this." Ben unhooked a large bundle of rope netting from the side of the wagon and started to walk toward the top of the hill, near the popcorn tree. "That's the best rise over there." Jarrod grabbed the largest burning stick from the fire and hurried to catch up.

A few minutes later, they made it to the top. Ben continued down over the far side of the rise, and began to spread out the net. Then he crouched down, out of sight, so anyone—or anything—coming up over the hill would not see him.

"Good luck."

"You too." Jarrod gathered his courage, held the burning torch up high, and began to walk down along the crest of the hill. He kept his eyes on the ground, making a mental note of every stick, hole, rock, and clump of grass. If he later forgot just one of these and tripped, it could cost him his life.

Minutes later, about three hundred feet away from his father, the boy stopped. He crouched, set the torch down into the soil, and slowly rolled it. As the last flames smothered, the moonlit darkness settled in.

"Your night has been reclaimed," Jarrod whispered slowly to the blackness behind him. "Humans don't belong here, just you and the moon and the darkness. Come for me, come for me now. I am the intruder in your darkness. Come for me."

The boy was instantly afraid, his chest quivering with his next breath. The more he imagined what was out in the blackness behind him, the more afraid he became. He strained his eyes to see what he knew was out there. The most chilling thought was of how exciting the day had been. Extra energy would go into the creation, and that meant they would be stronger and faster than before. If they were too strong, he might not be able to outrun them.

Jarrod wanted to bolt away that second, but held himself down. He strained to see them coming, his imagination stretching to its limits to give substance to what was just beyond the night's black curtain.

There came a sound then—a kind of barking snap, as if from some enraged wolf as it crushed its jaws down upon the head of some helpless prey. A frenzied squeal came next, followed by a thunderous bellow. And then the eyes appeared—huge orange disks hurtling nearly ten feet above the ground. The eyes were close—too close—and coming on fast. Jarrod sprang upward and began to flee for his life.

Heart pounding and breath exploding from his lungs, the ten year old ran faster through the night than he had ever run before, and it was still too slow. He leaped over obstacles he had planned to step around, and still the dark thing gained on him. Except for the eyes, it was made of pure blackness, what Jarrod imagined to be the substance of hell.

The more terrified the boy became, the more substance the dark thing seemed to gain. It was as hungry as pure evil could be, and sucked in the fear. Soon, bushes moved and dust swirled upward in the moonlight as its wagon-sized form hurtled past. It kept gaining on the tiny, puny boy. What started as dozens of yards shrunk to several. Its next bellow was an explosion of uncontrolled hatred, made even more frenzied by its hope that an eternal hunger was about to be satisfied.

A foul-smelling breath surrounded the fleeing boy, and he began to choke. He had only a few seconds left to go, and cried out, "It's here!" just before diving down over the rise near the top of the hill. With a dusty thud and loud, "Oomph," the ten year old landed beside his poised father. Ben rose and gave a mighty heave, hurling the top of the net as high into the air as he could. The dark thing, unable to do anything but follow the rising terrain, appeared an instant later above them.

Beast and net merged with a bloodcurdling scream of surprise. Jarrod flung himself upward and raced after his father, who tried frantically to grab hold of the four ropes trailing from the corners of the net.

"Hurry!" the running man yelled, finally getting hold of the last rope. The dark thing continued on a slightly rising path through the night, getting further above the downward slope on the far side of the hill. Jarrod caught up just as the ground ran out, and grabbed hold of the two ropes his father held out to him. Man and boy let out yells of delight as the ground dropped away and they sailed out into the darkness.

"Was it just this one?" Ben asked, nervous excitement in his voice.

"I think. I didn't have time to turn around and count them! Look how it fills the net all by itself! Hope it doesn't go too far. I don't think I can hold on."

"You better hold on. We're getting pretty high!"

The two and the dark thing were nearly a hundred feet above the ground, and close to three hundred feet from the top of the hill. Soon, the creature began to dissolve back into the darkness from which it came. The net began to deflate and sink downward. A few more minutes passed.

"Hope we don't end up in the trees," Jarrod said, still breathing hard from the running and the excitement.

"Looks like we're gonna hit that clear spot. Hold on." The two swung their legs upward to clear the tops of some low trees along the edge of a clearing, then made a running stop as the net dropped slowly back to earth. Both released their ropes and watched the net continue along on its own. The dark thing it held shrunk down past the size of a large bucket, rolled around and squeaked a few times, and then was gone.

"That was great," Jarrod shouted, running to collect the net. He dragged it back to his father, and both folded it up. It was then past one o'clock in the morning. Tired but happy, the two started back toward camp.

Sleep came easily to the Blackwells. Even with the bright moon, a million stars were visible in the sky. There weren't many mosquitoes or other bugs, either.

A hungry woodpecker awakened Ben and Jarrod a few minutes after sunrise the following morning. The bird's uninterrupted—and very loud—hammering made it seem like it was trying to cut the whole tree down, not just probe its bark for insects.

"Can you shoot it?" Jarrod moaned, not wanting to awaken all the way.

"Nah, we should be gettin' up."

"Few more minutes?"

"Yeah." Ben drifted back as close to sleep as he could get with all the racket.

Jarrod tried too. What helped was he shifted slightly so his face was in the sun. There were few things he thought more wonderful than being snug and warm in a soft bedroll, with the new sun on his face. Through his closed eyelids, he saw warm orange and imagined himself adrift on a sea of spring wildflowers. He sighed deeply, taking in the first gentle breeze of the morning. Nothing he knew was more relaxing than the thick, sweet smells of the forest floor.

And then the woodpecker hit a particularly hard spot on the nearby tree. What had been a thunking sound became a cracking sound, easily capable of rousing anything within miles.

"Dang, that does it," Ben moaned, sitting up in his bedroll. He drew the pistol he always slept with at his side. Jarrod, still trying not to awaken all the way, slowly raised his hands up to cover his ears. Ben rubbed his eyes and took aim—and then the woodpecker flew away.

"Bang, bang," the groggy man pretended. He slipped the pistol back into its holster, looked around, and turned toward his son. "Now you know there weren't any dang bugs under that hardwood. No, that bird was doin' that on purpose."

"Go away."

"Yes, I believe it was an evil creature, Son. One sent down by heaven above to inflict misery on our miserable lives." Ben loved to pick on his son and had to try very hard to keep from laughing. His favorite routine was that of a demented preacher, seeing evil at every turn in their lives.

"Go away. I'm sleepy."

"Ah, only a coward—or the devil himself—begs. What be you, boy? Devil or coward? Was that your evil pet, that False Woodpecker of The Damned?"

"Okay, okay, you win. Just stop. Please stop." Jarrod flung off his covers and sat up on the bottom of the bedroll. His head hung down for a few seconds, but then he looked his father squarely in the eye. "I'll get up. But if I die of exhaustion today, it's your fault. Got that, your fault." The boy stood and walked over to the latrine. Without turning, he finished, "And when I do die of exhaustion, I'm going to send a hundred Woodpeckers of the Damned to torment you the rest of your wasted life." The only thing Ben could do was begin to laugh.

Breakfast consisted of fried bacon, beans, dry crackers, fresh berries picked in the woods, and coffee. Ferdinand ate his usual mix of straw and oats, followed by a few gallons of water. By eight o'clock, they were back on the Santiam Trail, heading east.

It would take the rest of the day to pass through Shaw, Aumsville, Stayton, Mehama, Mill City, and Gates, before reaching the much narrower turnoff leading to Opal Creek Mine. People in all the towns came out to greet the traveling magicians, except in Mehama. There, the recent passing of the mayor's wife had the town in an official day of mourning. To all the good people, the Blackwells promised to put on a show on their return trip.

Away from the side of the Santiam River, the terrain became much more steep. Opal Creek, which drained into the Santiam, was also the name of the valley through which it flowed. To reach the valley, it was necessary to traverse a number of hills, some large enough to be called mountains. Often, Jarrod and Ben had to step down from the wagon and help push it uphill.

The day's biggest victory came just after eight o'clock in the evening. It was then they passed over the rim of the last hill and into Opal Creek Valley. Ferdinand knew the hardest work was done and began to trot downhill. So tired was the horse that it began to stumble, and had to be slowed down by constant pressure on the reins and the brakes of the wagon.

The valley was like nothing either had seen before. Giant red cedar trees, some nearly six hundred years old, stretched upward over one hundred and fifty feet. Their companions in the fertile soil, the Douglas firs, towered fifty feet taller. It was a valley of living cathedrals, each majestic and invincible.

"You could drive the wagon straight through!" Jarrod exclaimed of the wide spacing between the massive trunks. Ben turned Ferdinand off the narrow trail and did just that. After a few dozen yards, the majesty of the place began to take hold, and they stopped.

"I could live here forever," Jarrod finally whispered.

"We'll camp here." They were below one of the largest of the Douglas firs, which was close to eight feet in diameter.

"Can you imagine living like the Indians, a part of all this?"

"It would be nice," Ben agreed.

Later, after a dinner of bacon, beans, dry crackers, and coffee, the two walked out a short distance from camp. Everything was quiet and soft and smelled of pine or cedar. Each footstep made a soft crunching sound, the needles of the current season pressing into those of hundreds past. Jarrod reached out and touched one of the silent giants. An energy—a feeling he could not describe—seemed to flow into him.

There was little talk in camp that night. The forest was of such ancient calm that human sounds seemed strangely out of place. Neither wanted to break the spell. They slept as peaceful a sleep as had ever been slept.

The first blast of a rifle shattered the quiet a few minutes after midnight. The bullet exploded the lantern hanging on the side of the wagon, instantly igniting a fire. Five more shots followed in quick succession. Behind the blazing rifles, three men ran toward the camp.

Ben Blackwell dove out from his bedroll, turned, and began to fire the pistol he always slept with at his side. His first shot struck one of the men squarely in the chest, hurtling him back several feet to the ground. The other two men took cover behind the same huge tree and continued to fire their rifles. Ben fired two more times, but missed.

By then, Jarrod had escaped his own bedroll and taken cover behind the wagon. Ben was there a moment later. On the opposite side, flames spread up the thin wooden shell. In a few seconds, the top started to burn. When one of the men made a dash for a closer tree, Ben fired three more times. The man stopped in mid stride, hit so hard by two of the bullets that he spun around twice before dropping to the ground. It was then Jarrod saw that his father could not reload the pistol.

"Hurry!" the boy cried.

"I can't. Get under and imagine a tunnel. A deep, safe tunnel. Do it!" In the growing light of the blaze, Ben's wounded chest glistened a dark red. When his son reached out to help, the man used his last bit of strength to push him down under the wagon. "Do it now!"

Tears flowing from his eyes, the boy squatted down and began to sift his hands through the loose, dry soil. Out of the corner of his eye, he saw his father try to reach up into the front of the wagon, to grab their rifle. It was too late, though, and he slumped backward and slowly sprawled out onto the ground. Jarrod turned, and they looked at each other, only a few feet apart. Ben tried to say something, but it wasn't loud enough to be heard above the growing roar of the flames. Then he became still.

"No!" What sound did rise above the fire echoed in the darkened woods. Then Jarrod saw the boots of the third man. They came around the wagon and stopped a few yards behind his father's body. In slow circles, the boy's hands still sifted the soil. Some thought remained of the tunnel, but his focus was on the boots.

The man squatted down to look under the wagon. He was young and dirty and had eyes without conscience. On his head was the tattered remains of a Rebel cap. In an instant of feeling everything at once, the ten year old knew his father's assassin was a Confederate deserter who had been on the run for several years. Even though the war was over, this man continued to live by preying on others.

The two stared at each other for several seconds. Then the man grinned coldly and pointed his rifle. They were so close that aiming wasn't necessary. The roar of the fire had turned into a thunder. As flames began to leak through the bottom, the top of Jarrod's hair began to smoke.

Much seemed to happen during that next instant. Feelings of wanting to die with his father gave way to feelings of wanting to live. The awareness of creating the tunnel was still there, but in the background. What Jarrod wanted most was for the man to die, but he realized it was too late to fight back. A fragment of a vision of revenge just started to form—and then the ground gave way, the wagon collapsed, and the rifle discharged.

Jarrod tumbled down a steep incline. His scalp was bleeding from the scrape of the passing bullet, and flaming pieces from the wagon were everywhere. Some tumbled along with him, deeper and deeper underground, but he soon rolled clear. Seconds later, he crashed into a wall of cold earth and was stunned. His last memory was of looking up, past the trail of burning debris, to the bright glow at the mouth of the tunnel. Something else was there too, something large and shiny and moving upward at a very fast rate, but he couldn't hold onto consciousness long enough to see what it was.

Above ground, Elijah Burke tumbled backward, propelled by the recoil of his rifle and the outward rush of sparks and searing heat. Events happened too quickly for him to see the boy escape, and he figured him to be underneath the raging fire. A cruel smile came to his lips.

Elijah picked himself up, brushed off some of the dirt, and tried to think of a way of getting to Ben's body before it too was consumed by the fire. The killer wanted the clothes and anything that might be in the dead man's pockets. He started to approach, shielding his face from the intense heat—then caught a glimpse of something moving within the fire.

Out of the flames rose a snakelike creature as thick around as a man and twice as tall. Its flesh was hard, as if made of bending stone, and its head was massive. Huge jaws hungrily opened and closed, its foot-long fangs and razor-sharp teeth scissoring together so tightly they made loud scraping sounds.

The monster stared for a moment through its coal-black eyes, then screeched out and lunged. Elijah barely had time to begin his scream before being impaled, nearly cut in half, and lifted into the fire. He hung there for a few seconds, eight feet above the ground, then crashed down into the flaming remains of the wagon as the beast dissolved back into eternity.

CHAPTER THREE

# One Hundred and Thirty Years Later

Things were looking up for Victor, Jill, and Tony Magellan. The parents and son were a creative team who loved to invent, build things, program computers, and just generally enjoy anything that was fun, neat, and exciting. The problem was they hardly ever earned any money.

Mostly, they figured their lack of earnings was due to being ahead of their time. People weren't ready to buy whatever it was the three were selling, even though they probably would have been better off if they did. That's why the demonstration for the Child Support Unit of the Adult and Child Services Division was so important.

Like most state agencies, the ACSD was fifteen years behind the times when it came to computers. Office automation to them was having personal computers on every desk so employees could write their own memos. Right beside the PC's were the terminals which were connected to the agency's mainframe computers. Information was looked up on the terminals, written down on paper, then typed back into some program running on the PC's.

The Magellans had developed something they called Easylink, which was an easy way of hooking up a PC in place of a terminal, and getting rid of the terminal. Their software package was mainly a large collection of other people's software, which they changed slightly so it all worked together.

Jill was busy with something else, so Victor and Tony were going to conduct the demonstration. They tried to be calm and cheerful. Of the six agency people there, Loren

Bell made them the most nervous. He was the administrator of the division and was close to retirement. That meant he was old enough never to have learned about computers when he was in school. Mr. Bell still didn't believe in them but was at least willing to listen.

Carma Jones was a Supervising Caseworker. She was about fifty, really smart, and had been with the agency for fifteen years. What encouraged Victor and Tony most about Carma was her commitment to helping her employees. Her main goal was to remove as much of the repetitive, manual paper pushing from their jobs as possible so they could concentrate on analyzing and making decisions.

The other four, James Castor, Gary Leeper, LeAnn Randall, and Diane Cooper, were Child Support Caseworkers. Their jobs were to keep child support accounts accurate. This was easier said than done, especially when people didn't pay what they were supposed to.

"I guess we're ready," Victor started when all six had gathered around the table he was sitting at. Tony was behind the table, to help with the cable connections. "What I've got here is an IBM Laptop 10, which has a Pentium chip, twelve megabytes of memory, a one-gigabyte optical drive, and an adaptor board so it can hook up to your mainframe."

Victor opened the lid of the small PC, and the bright color screen came on. He slid it next to the terminal, and Tony began to unscrew one wire from the back of the terminal.

"What Tony will do is unhook the coaxial cable from the terminal and connect it to the laptop." They waited for the twelve year old to complete the connection. "Okay, now all you do is type in Easy, and press Enter." Immediately, the Magellan's special mix of programs began to operate.

"The first thing the software does is establish a link with your mainframe, and identify the computer as a terminal. In this case, we'll use the ID number of the one we just disconnected. Then it will determine which mainframe you have or combination of mainframes—and establish link libraries to them. All a link library is, is a translation table. If you want to print, the software looks up what command means 'Print' to your mainframe, and sends that. That takes about ten seconds...and then, you're ready."

Tony came back around the table and sat down beside his father. He felt like a magician about to do tricks for an audience.

"Okay, that was the hard part." Tony paused, to give anyone a chance to chuckle. LeAnn did, and both Magellan's breathed an inner sigh of relief. Even one chuckle was a very good sign. "Okay..." The boy noticed his father lightly tap his right index finger on the table, a signal that meant he was repeating a word or saying a word that was just filling in time. "One of your records is called 'SMUX'. You see the program asking you to enter the name of one of your records, so you just type in 'SMUX' like this..."

As soon as Tony keyed in the four letters, the program called that record from the mainframe and displayed it on the screen.

"Okay..." There was another finger tap. "Ahm..." Another tap by Victor. "The program will now go from field to field and ask which codes you enter when you want to update them on the mainframe. It stopped on 'Name'. What do you enter if you want to change the name?"

"You have to go in on the 'PZZYP1' file," Carma answered.

Victor laughed, "That's as intuitive a name as I've ever heard. How on earth did your programmers come up with that one?"

"We'll never know," James laughed back. "It was set up twenty years ago, and that programmer is long gone."

"So I'll just enter 'PZZYP1', and then the program will go on to the next field. What file do you access when you want to update the address?"

"LOP2B4," Loren replied dryly, obviously displeased that their computer system was laughed at. Victor and Tony tried to keep a straight face, and almost made it—but then Tony started to grin. He tried to think of other things, like getting stung by a wasp, but it did no good. He started to get really warm. The suit and tie, which he hardly ever wore, began to feel like a goose down parka. Finally, he just lost it and began to laugh.

"I'm sorry," he finally managed to say. "I'm not mocking your system, it's just that ..."

"We call that one 'Lop-Two-Before'," Diane laughed. By then, everyone except Mr. Bell was on the verge of hysteria as the silliness of their naming conventions became so apparent.

"But no one has ever figured out before what," Gary roared, bending over. When he was finally able to control his laughing, he straightened back up and continued, "Please don't fire me, Mr. Bell. I have a wife and two kids."

After that, the rest was easy. Amid much laughter and joking, Tony managed to get and enter the individual, very oddball file names of the twenty other fields which appeared on SMUX. When it was all done, he pressed a single key.

"That's all there is to it," Victor explained proudly. "Now, anything you change on here will be automatically sent back to the mainframe, without your having to go into the individual subfiles." He and Tony began to trade off giving parts of the explanation, meshing like well-oiled gears.

"We can also pick out special fields, like this phone number. With a modem and a telephone hookup, just selecting that field will automatically dial that number. If it's busy, it will try again every five minutes or some other interval you decide. If you want, you can even type in a message you want to give the person who answers the phone."

"You'd use that feature if you received another call and wanted to look at another SMUX, and still keep trying to get through on the first call. The program translates your typed message into a nice-sounding computer voice, so you can tell whomever answers who you are and ask them to please wait for a few seconds until you can get to them."

"There really isn't a limit to how much you can have running in the background," Tony went on. "Anytime anything happens with some process you have there, the program pops open a window to let you know."

The rest of the demonstration went flawlessly. Soon, the six were sitting down, coming up with one idea after another about how much easier their work could be. About the only thing the Magellans regretted was their software made things look so easy that it didn't appear there was much to it. They wanted to brag about the tens of thousands of lines of handwritten code they sweated out during the last three years, about all the negotiating they had done with the software companies whose products they built into their own. Mainly, they wanted to brag about their inventive, imaginative approach to designing Easylink from a worker's, not a programmer's, point of view.

In the end, all that really mattered was they knew how good they were. Even Mr. Bell came around and seemed to get caught up in the enthusiasm of his employees. Two hours later, they had an agreement to install one complete test workstation. Six months after that, if all went well, they had a tentative agreement for twenty more. It was the first big contract the Magellan team had ever gotten.

Victor and Tony concluded the demonstration and left. They were calm and poised—until the fourth floor elevator door closed. Then they went nuts, jumping up and down, shaking hands, and hugging each other. Words couldn't express what they were feeling, so actions took over. When the elevator stopped on the second floor to let more people in, they barely had time to compose themselves. Down on the first floor, the two walked as proudly as two partners could.

"Have to take a leak?" Victor asked.

"A leak? I'm so excited I could poop my guts out."

"Do the leak first. You need the practice."

"Yeah! The way I feel, I could do a royal one on the fifty yard line during half-time at the Super Bowl." Tony was referring to his training program, of sorts, to learn to urinate in public restrooms. He was okay when the urinals had dividers between them, but couldn't do a drop if they were open. Worse were the open troughs found in some really old restrooms. If the toilets were occupied, the twelve-year old risked explosion and death before being able to start the flow.

The two were in luck. The restroom was crowded and had urinals without dividers. Even better, the door and paper towel dispensers made loud noises when used. If the boy could do it there, the boy would be a man who could do it anywhere. Victor tucked the laptop computer under his arm and approached the urinals with his son. In mock seriousness, they spoke.

"Good luck."

"Thanks, Pop." The moment of truth had arrived. Zippers came down, aim was taken—and Tony did it! "Yes!" Two other men looked over, and Victor gave them a proud grin.

"Mine was fourteen before he could," one man commented. "Congratulations, son." Two other men at the sinks turned. One gestured with his hands at Victor, who gave an approving nod in response. Then all the men in the restroom began to applaud. Tony turned bright red, but was able to keep on going.

On the way to the car, the two loosened their ties and unbuttoned their top shirt buttons.

"Hungry?" Victor asked.

"You bet."

"How about something special, at the Black Angus?"

"All right!"

In the car, the first thing they heard on the radio was, "This is a CBS Radio special announcement. We join Claire Jennings at the Capitol.... 'This is Claire Jennings reporting live from Washington, DC. Well, it's official. Flat-Rate is now the law. In a narrow three vote victory, the Congress just minutes ago made the fifteen-percent flat-rate tax the law of the land. No more deductions, exemptions, subtractions, writeoffs or loopholes. If you earn it, you'll pay fifteen percent of it. Proponents of the measure are expected to rally here shortly for a weenie roast, using—you guessed it—several copies of the current nine-thousand-page Internal Revenue Codes as fuel for the fire. This is ...'"

Victor flipped off the radio, let out a yell of delight, and blared the horn several times.

"Yes, they did it, they actually did it!" The thirty-six year old had to sit back in the bucket seat to catch his breath. Tony just smiled. "You know what this means, kid? It means this wacked-out, screwed-up, over-taxed, overly-complicated mess of country is finally getting somewhere. Jeez, next we'll be hearing the deficit is under ten trillion! Come on, let's go eat." Victor started the car, checked for traffic, and pulled out.

"You know what we should do?" Tony asked. "Buy some lottery tickets. If there is a lucky day for us, this is it."

"Good idea. God, this is great. I mean really great. You know, I don't mind telling you. There were times—I mean a lot of times—when I just about gave up. I'd almost feel it was a curse to be creative and want to do all these crazy projects. I used to actually dream about being normal. You know, getting up in the morning and going to a regular job, earning a regular paycheck. When we had you, it was even more that way. I didn't want our son growing up screwed-up because he never had a daddy with a regular job." Tony just smiled.

"Really. Here comes little Freddy Kruger because there might not be a pay check next month." After a quick pause, and with even more excitement, Victor continued, "You know what, we should stop and get something really nice for Jill. If it wasn't for her, we wouldn't be here today, kid. All her working, all her support—not to mention all her stress. You got a wonderful mom, Tony, you really do."

The prime rib lunch was great. They even splurged and had the fried zucchini as an appetizer. On the way to the biggest shopping mall in town, the two spotted Eddie, Victor's brother, going the opposite way in traffic. Eddie was a police detective and had been part of the Salem Police Department for ten years. Victor honked his horn, and his brother honked back.

"Too bad Eddie doesn't have kids. If I were a kid, I'd love to have an uncle like me and a cousin like you."

"I'm glad you're not getting too full of yourself."

"Hey, why not? We earned it. Okay, now what about Jill? What's that little creeper been wanting lately?"

CHAPTER FOUR

# Meeting Ophelia

The Magellans lived six miles east of town, off of Highway 22. The highway was known as the Santiam Trail in the old days. They had just under ten acres of land, most of it fields and woods.

Jill and Victor had built their house themselves. It was another of their creative projects which incorporated many unusual features. The basement walls, for example, had plastic reinforcing bar instead of steel, because steel would have eventually rusted and caused the concrete to crack. Walls were framed with galvanized steel two-by-fours, not wood, so they never had to worry about termites or carpenter ants. And the roof was made of tile, not shingles, so it would never have to be replaced.

There was also a shop, in which they worked on their larger projects. It was in the shop that Ophelia lived. She—or it—was the Magellan's most expensive, most exciting, and most terrifying project.

"Oh good, she's back," Tony said, spotting his mother's car as they pulled into the driveway. "You think she'll like it?"

"I think she's gonna go nuts, she'll like it so much. Okay, remember, play it cool."

"In here," Jill Magellan called from the kitchen when she heard her husband and son come in the front door. Victor put the present down on the sofa on their way through the living room.

"I made us some chocolate chip cookies just in case we have to console ourselves. Do we have to...console ourselves?" The two pretended to be real serious, even glum, about how the demonstration had gone. "Oh well, don't give it a second thought. Remember, you're dealing with the state." Jill took the first cookie from the plate on the table. "Did they like it at all?"

"They loved it!" Victor finally announced, unable to pretend any longer. He stepped over and hugged Jill, who immediately started to push him away.

"Don't try to hug me, you big rat. Coming in here all sad like they tossed you out. You're in big trouble. Don't try to make up." Jill turned away from Victor, but just for a few seconds. Then they hugged for real, and kissed each other.

"Goll, don't you guys have any decency?"

"Shut up, Anthony," Jill mumbled, still kissing Victor. She held out the cookie she had in her hand. "Mmmmm, take this and go chew on it somewhere."

"Thanks a bunch." When Tony reached over and took the cookie, Jill broke away from Victor and grabbed him instead. In an instant, she was hugging her son.

"Ewww, yuck!" the boy protested.

"Congratulations, you little rat." Then she let him go and stood back. "So tell me all about it."

The telling took as long as it takes three excited people to consume a plateful of chocolate chip cookies. The two enjoyed recreating the highlights of the demonstration and didn't hesitate to exaggerate a bit about how impressed the others were. Then, they decided to go out and work on Ophelia.

"Huh, what's this?" Victor asked casually as the three started through the living room.

"You got me a present!" Jill sat down on the sofa. Victor picked up the beautifully wrapped box and handed it to her.

Like a kid at Christmas, the thirty-five year old tore into it. In a few seconds, she opened the lid and saw the dress.

"My dress! You got my dress!" Bubbling with excitement, Jill stood and held it up to herself. "It's beautiful. You got my dress!" Then a bit of reality crept in, and she all of a sudden looked serious. "You shouldn't have. We can't afford this. I was only looking at it. You shouldn't have." After a long, loving look at the two, and a deep sigh, she smiled again and finished, "But I'm glad you did. The hell with the cost. I deserve it."

"Thank you, Vicky. Thank you, Tony." Jill gave them both quick hugs, then carefully draped the dress over the back of the sofa.

Even Tony was impressed and said, "I don't care much for dresses myself, but I'd call that a definite magnitude seven—especially the way it will look on you."

"Yeah," Jill agreed, stepping back to admire the $700 piece of sophisticated fashion. After a few more seconds, she said, "Ah, where were we? Oh yeah, Ophelia. Come on, this is our day for everything."

A little more than a third of the shop was taken up by an old truck trailer which had been converted into The Horror Box. This was a prototype of a carnival amusement. Once it was perfected, the Magellans hoped to manufacture and sell more of them to amusement operators around the world.

The front of The Horror Box trailer was a giant light board twice as tall as the trailer. The top of the board was hinged so it could fold down when the trailer was moved. All of the lights on the board were controlled by a computer inside the trailer. When the lights were on, the board looked like a huge computer display.

Attached to the center of the light board was a wooden box big enough to hold two sitting people. Creaky wooden steps led up to the box. The back of the box opened into a chamber inside the trailer. In this chamber is where Ophelia lived.

Tony started up the stairs, Victor stepped up into the trailer to operate the computer, and Jill stayed outside to watch what was happening.

"Stairs sound really great," Tony said. "Maybe we won't even need the amplifier."

"I think we should keep it," Jill answered. "Remember, at a carnival or fair, there will be lots of noise. The squeaking is good in here, but probably no one would be able to hear it outside."

"Yeah, probably." Tony opened the side door to the actual box part of The Horror Box, crouched down, and stepped inside. "Ready," he called out.

"Ready in here," Victor called from inside the trailer. "Here we go."

A few seconds later, the light board came on. Tens of thousands of different colored lights made a picture of an enormous spider web. Jill started humming the scary music that would have been playing in the background if it would not have prevented them from hearing one another.

"Looking great." Then the box started to shake slightly. The picture adjusted itself so it looked as though the entire web was shaking. Suddenly, the tips of giant spider legs appeared on top, as if a massive arachnid had been alerted to the capture of prey. The legs twitched and hesitated, feeling the vibrations of the web—and then the beast seemed to lunge over the top edge, onto the web, and scurry toward the box. It was all an animated picture, but looked frighteningly real.

Jill screamed, and Tony screamed back as the huge spider seemed to crawl in behind the box.

"Oh yeah, audience participation is a must. Imagine all these people on line screaming out when they see her heading for the box. Then the two in the box scream back because they know what's about to happen. Oh yeah, just right."

Inside the box, Tony braced. Even though he had been through it a hundred times, the experience of being a spider's victim still sent chills through his spine. He was seated in front of a narrow counter, on which was a bowl of slime and four pretend spider egg halves, each about as big as half of a soccer ball.

As Tony slowly drew in his breath, he heard the creaking of a trap door in the back of the box. It was dark and cool in there, what he imagined a spider's lair to be like. Without warning, the clawed tips of two giant legs reached up onto the back side of the counter. These weren't a picture, but the real thing. They felt and scraped. The boy wanted to pull away, but there was nowhere to go.

"Mmmmm, what tasty morsel have we here?" came the evil voice then, as old and craggy as time. "What's the matter, my precious little tidbit—spider got your tongue?" All at once, the mechanical monster leaped upward into full view. This was Ophelia, a cross between a spider and an alien. Her body was bloated and covered with coarse dark hairs and spines, but her head and face were vaguely humanlike.

Gruesome red eyes, thick with scum, bulged and twitched. Her mouth gaped open, unable to close around two rows of three-inch-long, needlelike fangs. Shiny ribbons of venom trickled down from her mouth. With every breath she wheezed and choked. In all, Ophelia was about as large as a refrigerator.

"Ah, that's what I like, quiet little morsels. Quiet ones are more tender, you know. Less gristle. But quiet ones also make Ophelia very angry—because they don't speak!"

The last part of the sentence was screeched out, and the beast lunged to within a foot of the cowering boy.

"Talk to me, my next meal. Talk to Ophelia before she drains your blood."

"Ah, what should I...ah, say..."

"My name is Ophelia, you miserable, edible wretch! Address me by my name or I shall have your head!" The combination of screech and wheeze was so intense that little droplets of venom flung outward. Then the horrid creation settled back a bit and chuckled.

"I can see you won't be any fun. Might as well get on with the feeding. No need to tell you to relax—once my venom flows into you, you'll be paralyzed. That's very relaxed!" Ophelia screeched with laughter.

"Is there anything you'd like to say for yourself before I devour you, my doomed...?"

"Ah, wait a minute. Dad, I think on that sentence, she's supposed to say 'doomed victim.' Dad?"

"I heard you. Hang on. Yeah, you're right. Let me try it again. Just a second." There was a brief pause as the automatron's voice programming was adjusted. Then it continued speaking.

"Is there anything you'd like to say for yourself before I devour you, my doomed victim?"

"Ah, yes. Yes, Ophelia. I'd like to bet you for my life." The beast moved inward again, poised as if ready to strike. It's eyes glared at Tony.

"A bet? Mmmm, how interesting. Continue."

"Let me hide something under one of these eggs. If you can find it, in two tries, I'm yours. If you can't find it, you let me go."

"An even chance. I like that. All right, my frightened little bit of human flesh, I accept. But what shall you hide?" The giant claw reached upward, as if to strike the boy, but then dropped down to just above the bowl of slime. The claw opened, releasing a simulated human eye. It plopped into the slime, and Ophelia cackled.

"I hope you don't mind. It was left over from my last victim. One who lost his bet!" The mechanical creature withdrew and was soon out of sight.

Tony hated the fake slime. He hesitated, then reached into the bowl and plucked out the fake eyeball. The slime stuck to it, and a big stretch of it pulled up out of the bowl. The boy wiped it free with his finger, and the stretch snapped back like a loose, wet, slimy rubber band.

"You're not afraid of the slime, are you?" Ophelia asked from the darkness behind the box.

"No, no, Ophelia. I'm not afraid."

"Then be quick about it! My patience grows thin!"

Tony selected one of the four egg halves and concealed the fake eyeball.

"Ah, I'm done." An instant later, the evil creature lunged back into the box and reared above Tony. It was so big, only its front legs and head could actually fit into the box. Slowly, it began to look at the egg halves. It sniffed them, held its claws above them—and finally decided on the one to turn over. The rubbery, oozing mechanical mouth smiled a bit as the right claw slowly grasped and lifted the third egg half. There was nothing under it.

"Ophelia hates to lose! It makes her very, very angry!" It turned back and examined the remaining three halves. "Mmmmm, where could the little trickster have put my precious eye? Could it be...here?" The beast turned over the egg half which concealed the fake eyeball. A bone-chilling screech of delight filled the box and as she prepared to make her final, killing lunge.

"Come to Ophelia, come to Ophelia..." Tony reacted quickly and escaped out the other side of the box. There was a slide there, which led down through the trailer and ended in the back. In a few seconds, the boy was safely on the ground behind the trailer. He hurried around to join his mother in the front.

From the front, it couldn't be seen that Tony had escaped. If they were a real audience waiting in line, they would think he was still up inside. There was a loud scream from the box, which began to shake and tremble, as if a great fight were going on within. Ophelia's screaming could be heard too, along with violent thrashing and tearing. Then the box became still. Loud sucking noises came next, and then more silence.

Finally, about ten seconds later, a door opened in the bottom of the box and a simulated, web-wrapped body dropped out and fell to the ground. It looked like that of a young boy. Ophelia's evil cackling was heard, and then her picture appeared on the giant light board. Her image left the box, climbed back up to the top of the web, and went over the edge to hide on the other side. Victor came out from the trailer a few moments later and joined the other two.

"Things went perfectly inside. That new voice-recognition program is amazing. It actually interpreted everything you said as fast as you said it."

"The response look-up went fast, too," Tony noted. "I couldn't even tell there was any delay between when I said something and when she answered."

"And the board looked great," Jill added.

"Well then, that's it for this part. Now what about the body on the ground?"

Tony said, "Definitely have to drop it into something, so it can be brought back up into the trailer for the next time. You can't have some operator pick it up and carry it back up."

"No, but you could have the hangman pick it up and then dump it into a chute in the trailer." The hangman was who they envisioned would operate the amusement. This would be some great big guy dressed in an executioner's cowl who would lead the victims up the creaking steps to the box. Jill stepped over and pretended to be the hangman.

"Yeah, I think that would work. Think of the theatrics that could be involved. He'd come over, pick up the body—or two bodies if there were two in the ride—and then stuff them in here." Jill picked up the phony human remains and motioned as though there were an opening in the trailer in which to drop them. "The audience would boo him, and he could scowl back or say something crude. Yeah, I think something like picking up and disposing of the bodies would make him be hated more."

"Might be," Victor halfway agreed.

"I agree with Mom. I think that's a great idea. Not to mention easier than a conveyor outside the trailer. If it were inside, we could just have a belt thing..." The boy wasn't sure of the exact mechanical description and just motioned with his hands.

"Okay then. Let's do it," Victor said. Jill dropped the rather grotesque remains, wiped her hands clean, and went back over to the others.

"There, I've done my work for the day. I'm going in to try on a certain new dress certain devoted admirers of mine recently purchased."

"Purchased? She thinks we'd actually spend that much money on her." The two guys looked at each other.

"There's a sucker born every minute, Dad."

"Well, we'll let her think that, at least until the cops come looking."

"Oh, right, you shoplifted it? Right. Like you'd look so guilty you wouldn't make it out of the store. Nice try, fellas. You'd have spent twice that if it was something I wanted—and felt honored." Jill gently pinched Victor on his left cheek, and hurried toward the door of the shop.

"So, how we gonna build that conveyor?" Victor asked.

"First, I think we got to cut a hole about there..."

CHAPTER FIVE

# Tony Meets a Very Old Friend

One of the neatest things about the Magellan property was the Southern Pacific railroad tracks a short distance behind it. They weren't close enough to cause a nuisance up at the house but were fairly easy to walk to. Tony loved watching the trains go by and frequently squished pennies and other coins on the tracks. The tracks were good for experiments too, although he doubted the folks at the company would see it that way.

Two current experiments were the Rail Racer and Rail Bike. The racer was a model racing car with magnetic wheels and a real jet engine. The bike was a regular two-wheeler with extra-wide rims, no tires, and a fiberglass cowling to reduce wind drag.

That morning, Tony was going to test the racer. Since the last one had blown up, this one was all new. The day was bright and warm, perfect for being out along the tracks. Before getting started, the boy just sat on the rail and enjoyed being there. As far as he could see in both directions, the rails cut a neat path through the woods and curved off into the distance. Even though he knew what lay beyond, he liked to imagine it was something different and more exciting.

Finally, the time was right. Tony pulled a stethoscope out from his pack, put it on, and listened to one rail. Silence. Even if a train were just out of hearing distance, he would have a full fifteen minutes. Quickly, he unstowed the racer and set it onto the rail. The magnetic wheels clamped down solidly. Fuel was next, a full quarter cup. Then he clipped on the battery to the starter motor and engine glow plug, and set the brake.

Tony held his breath, flipped the starter switch, and took off running away from it as fast as he could. He had to make at least one hundred yards before the automatic brake let go. The racer was at its fastest then and offered the most thrilling view as it wooshed past.

Running on the bed of crushed rock was murder on his ankles, but the twelve year old pushed as hard as he could. Fifty yards stretched to seventy-five, and then to one hundred. At that distance, he could no longer hear the whine of the electric starter motor. What he was starting to hear was the combination woosh and whistle of the eight-inch-long jet engine as it came up to full power.

The Rail Racer reached a full-power scream and began to quiver on the rail. Suddenly, the automatic brake let go, and it was off. Zero to sixty miles per hour took a little under six seconds. Tony stepped back a bit, to avoid certain death if it jumped out of control or exploded, and cheered as it screeched past. He should have covered his ears but didn't, so as not to diminish his full appreciation of its fantastic power.

A few seconds and another several hundred feet down the tracks, the fuel ran out and the small parachute automatically deployed. There was one last backfire and puff of smoke, then silence as the small projectile dragged to a stop.

Immediately, Tony took off down the tracks, to retrieve his creation. It stopped about a hundred yards away. For the first few dozen yards, until the gentle breeze blew it away, the aroma of hotly-combusted fuel hung in the air. There was nothing more exciting to him than that smell mixed with those of oil, creosote, various weed-killing chemicals, and the surrounding woods.

The distant clapping of hands caught Tony's attention as he approached the racer. There, up on a hill about fifty yards away, was a boy sitting in front of a small tent. He didn't look familiar. Casually, Tony started up.

As Tony approached the boy through the dry, waist-high grass, the other boy stood. He was about twelve also but wearing really unusual clothes. The shorts and shoes looked like they were made of leather, and the short-sleeved shirt and socks like they were embroidered silk. The pattern was really bright and large. To Tony, the stranger looked like a cross between someone living in the Swiss Alps and a Gypsy.

"Nice run. Must have hit at least seventy."

"Oh, probably more like sixty. Thanks. You from around here?"

"No. Just passing through, sort of."

"Oh. Great tent. What kind?" Tony stepped closer to look at the tent, but the other boy blocked him from looking inside, while trying not to make it look like a block.

"Ah, I don't know. Just a tent."

"Looks like Kevlar," Tony said, smoothing his hand along the top. "Man, a bulletproof tent."

"Good for camping out in Iran."

"Yeah. Ah, I'm Tony, Tony Magellan. I live up there."

"My name is Jarrod, ah, Blackwell."

"Your dad around somewhere?"

"No, ah, I'm alone."

"Oh. Where you from?"

"Sort of by Gates."

"My dad and I go fishing up there sometimes. Nice place."

"Yeah. So, ah, mind showing me your Rail Racer?"

“Sure, come on.” Tony turned and took a few steps back down the grassy hillside. “Hey, how’d you know what I call it?”

“Just a guess. I mean that’s kind of what it does.”

“Yeah.” Tony kept on going. Jarrod was a bit hesitant at first, then caught up to him.

“Gonna be a great day ...” Suddenly, the sound of a train horn froze both of them.

“Crap! My racer!” Tony took off in a run, and Jarrod followed. Almost immediately, Tony tripped in the tall grass and fell. Jarrod kept going, made it to the tracks, then sprinted for the racer.

The six-engine freight train was bearing down at close to fifty miles per hour. When the engineer saw what was happening, he began to blare the horn. Jarrod continued his sprint, dove down into the crushed rock, reached, and flipped the racer off the rail—just as the first engine thundered past.

The engineer opened the side window, leaned out, and angrily waved his fist. He also shouted something which could not be heard over the roar of the other engines. Jarrod was scuffed but okay. He rolled down into the dirt beside the tracks, sat up, and began to smooth his right hand up and down on his scraped left arm.

When he finally got there, the first things Tony saw were a few red blood stains on the rocks beside the rail. Scared, he hurried over to Jarrod. They had to shout to hear each other above the noise from the passing freight cars.

“You okay?”

“Fine.” Tony extended his hand, and helped the other boy up. There wasn’t a scratch on him. Jarrod quickly turned, picked up the Rail Racer, and handed it to Tony. Then he began to brush off his shorts and shirt, which had gotten quite dirty.

"Thanks. Wanna go back?" Jarrod nodded that he did, and they both started along the side of the tracks. Soon, the last car clacked by.

"You remember when they used to have cabooses?"

"Yeah. About when we moved here, they got rid of them and started putting those little radio boxes on the back."

"I think it would be great to ride in a caboose."

"Yeah."

"You buy that?"

"Oh, no, you can't buy anything like this. I made it—including the engine."

"Really. Wow."

"Yeah. I call it a vapor jet. See, an engine this small is too small to have a real compressor stage. So you have to heat the fuel. I do that by putting the fuel inside the turbine shaft." Tony angled the model around so Jarrod could see in the top of the engine.

"See how it's not a regular straight shaft, but like a bulb inside. It's hollow. That's the fuel tank. Once the flame starts to burn, when the starter motor is still going, it heats up the shaft. Pretty soon, the fuel inside starts to boil, and then it burns slicker than snot."

"Sounds a little dangerous."

"It is. Fuel vapor by itself won't burn, but add a little oxygen, and...Pow! My last one, a crack must have started in the shaft and let in air because it went up like a land mine. This one, I used a little bit softer steel. Not as brittle." Soon, they reached the pack and other supplies.

"Gonna do another run?"

"Not today. I'll tear it down and check everything first. Kind of like a fuel dragster." Jarrod watched as Tony packed everything away. The racer itself went in nose first, so the engine and back wheels stuck out.

"So, what are you gonna do?"

"I don't know. Hang around till I move on, I guess."

"You run away or something?"

"No."

"If you ran away, you can come with me. Maybe eat something before they catch you."

"I didn't run away, I said."

"Okay, okay." Tony slipped on the pack, secured it around his shoulders, and started toward home. "You can still come with me."

"Okay." Jarrod caught up, and the two walked beside each other.

It only took about five minutes to reach the back side of the Magellan's ten acres. There were no fences, just widely-spaced trees to mark the property line.

"Our border is all black walnut trees. In another ten or so years, they'll be big enough to make furniture out of. Ever dry wood to make furniture?" Jarrod shook his head that he hadn't, and Tony continued, "You paint the ends of the logs with tar, so they don't dry out too fast, then let them set for a few years. Then you cut them into boards."

"In the old days, we...I mean they, used to just cut them down and saw them up, and let them split if they had a mind to. Wow, look at the size of that praying mantis!" Jarrod pointed to a four-inch-long insect predator hopping across the grass tops to get out of their way. It used its wings to help, but didn't actually fly.

"My dad and I raise them in cages. Got this system all worked out where we put a deer pellet or something in this bottom thing and, when the flies come, some of them go up this one-way tube into the cage."

"Wow, a bug cage with an automatic supply of live flies."

"Moths, too. Mantes love moths. At night, we put a little bulb in place of the deer pellet, and the same thing happens. I'll show you when we get there."

"Make the cage too?"

"Oh, yeah. We make lots of things."

"Like what?"

"Our new thing is amusements. You know, like they set up at carnivals and state fairs and drive around in trucks."

"Oh, yeah, I know. What kinds of amusements?"

"We got this really neat new one. Call it The Horror Box. It's this..." Tony caught himself then and stopped walking. "Wait a minute. You're not one of these industrial spies, are you?"

"Me? No way. Just someone who's...well, passing through."

Tony continued walking, and said, "Then I still say you ran away. You live in Gates—if that's really where you live—and you're all alone camping out, what, thirty miles from home?" Jarrod could only shrug his shoulders.

The two boys came in the back way, across the field, and past the gardens.

"We've got about three quarters of an acre in gardens. We only use half each year, and let the other half lay fallow. All of it's been dug down and mulched about two feet. Stuff just goes crazy growing."

"God, it smells great."

"There's my dad." Tony waved to his father, who was out in front of the house, washing the car. Victor took a break from his chore as the boys approached.

"Hi," Jarrod said.

"Hello."

"Pop, this is Jarrod, ah, Jarrod Blackwell. He's camping out down by the tracks. Jarrod, this is my pop, Victor Magellan." The two shook hands.

"Nice to meet you, Jarrod. Your parents with you?"

Tony answered, "No, he lives in Gates, and he's alone, and he says he didn't run away."

"Well, then...I hope you'll join us for lunch."

"He's not an industrial spy either."

"Even better. Tell your mom I'll be about ten minutes."

The two boys headed for the house. Inside, in the kitchen, Jill was making lunch.

"Mom, this is Jarrod Blackwell. He didn't run away, and he's alone, and he's camping out down by the tracks. I asked him to have lunch with us. Dad will be about ten minutes."

"Hi, Jarrod. Welcome. I'll be about ten minutes then. Oh, and if you'd like, you can wash your clothes. Tony can find something else for you to wear."

Jarrod smiled, "Thanks, but I'll be cleaning them tonight anyway. Unless it's not okay to eat this way."

"Heavens no, you're fine."

"Okay." Jarrod smiled again, a little awkwardly, and followed Tony to his room in the back of the house.

"We can wash up, and I can show you some neat things. My parents are great. They let me do just about anything I want, as long as it doesn't blow up the house or escape at night and bite them."

CHAPTER SIX

# Tony's Lair

Tony's bedroom was an amazing place that looked more like a cave than a bedroom. One wall was stone, and the rest was wood paneling, except the back, which was mostly glass. In one area, about the size of a door, the glass was covered with window blinds. In one corner, hanging from the wall, was a large rope mesh ball with blankets inside.

"Behind there is my bat cave," the boy explained, slipping out of his pack and setting it down beside a cluttered wooden table. He went over and opened the blinds, revealing the inside of an actual small cave. Several dozen brown bats began to move on the walls and ceiling, disturbed by the light. Tony shut the blinds again.

"Light bothers them, so I look mostly when it's dark, with a red light." The twelve year old reached over and touched a large reflector telescope with a one-foot-diameter barrel. "I can see the rings of Saturn with this." Tony's next stop was his desk, on which was his computer.

"This awesome beast is an IBM System 4. It has four Pentium chips, sixty megabytes of RAM, another sixty megabytes of nonvolatile flash memory, one ten-gigabyte phase-change optical disk, and two three-and-a-half inch drives, not to mention the ultra-high resolution graphics card and this flat-panel screen. This is two thousand by two thousand pixels, with unlimited colors." The boy's voice nearly quivered as he described the system, and he had to take in a long, deep breath when he finished.

"You use it all?"

"Not most of the time, but there are some things, like the 3-D drafting programs and the animation programs that need it all. I'm just starting to write screenplays, and I'm trying to animate them too. Someday, I'm just gonna send a video cassette to a producer and let him sit down and watch my script instead of having to read through it."

"That could be good."

Tony sat down on the corner of his desk, and motioned for Jarrod to sit in the nice wood-and-leather chair. He did.

"Over there is a crossbow I built. I did it exactly the way they did in medieval times. It's a composite. The Arabs invented the method thousands of years ago." The twelve year old, getting more excited by the minute, jumped down, took the bow from the stone wall, and returned to sit back on the corner of the desk.

"See, when the bow is drawn, this side—the back—stretches, and this side—the belly—gets squeezed." Tony pointed to the various parts of the authentically-built weapon. "The both sides are glued together. To help the stretch, you use animal sinew. The best sinew is something called the ligamentum nuchae. It's the bundle that runs along the spine and over the shoulders of most mammals. To help the squeeze, you use animal horn, from a buffalo or a ram. The Arabs got so good at building these, they even figured out what the best glue was." Tony paused to catch his breath and see how well Jarrod was keeping up.

"If this is too weird..."

"No, go ahead. I love stuff like this."

"Anyway, the Arabs used glue made from the skin of the roof of the mouth of the Volga sturgeon. No kidding, the stuff's amazing."

"And you actually obtained all these...ingredients."

"Yup, and it wasn't easy, let me tell you." Tony jumped off and let Jarrod hold the crossbow. After a few seconds, he took it back, returned it to the wall, and took down another handmade item. This time, he just leaned on the desk during his enthusiastic explanation.

"This is my native blowgun. First, you find the wood—like a six-foot sapling. Then you split it down the middle, and dry and straighten the halves over a small fire so they fit perfectly together. Then you cut notches down both halves, so there's a little hole all the way through. Then you seal the two halves together with beeswax, wrap the whole thing in strips of wet bark, and let it dry out." Tony let Jarrod hold the six-foot-long blowgun.

"When the bark dries, it shrinks and squeezes the whole thing together really tight. Then the real work begins. You have to make the hole smooth on the inside, so you take a really long stick with some wet animal hide on the end, put gritty sand on the hide, and ram it down through the hole. After hours—and I mean hours and hours—you switch to a finer grit, and finally to really fine sand. It takes weeks."

"I imagine it would."

"Eventually, you get it smooth enough on the inside for the darts."

"Don't tell me. To make the darts, you use porcupine quills, poison steamed out of a jungle vine, and a wad of chewed animal hide on the end. When you load one, first you spit on the end to get the hide wet, then slide it in here and..." Jarrod raised the blowgun, pretended to load a poison dart, then puffed through the bottom end.

"Great," Tony laughed, taking back the blowgun. He returned it to its mount on the wall, then motioned Jarrod over. "You're as weird as me."

The two went over to an area of the wall where there were mounted animals. There was a raccoon, fox, and bobcat. All looked very lifelike, as if instantly frozen in some movement.

"Great work. Bet it cost you a bundle."

"Nope, I did them."

"Really? They're great."

"Yeah. I told you, I like to do lots of different things. Downstairs, there's this cutting tool, like a little router. It's hooked up to the computer. What I do on these is find a video tape of some wildlife show, find where they show, like a raccoon, and grab some of the scenes on the computer."

"Oh, so like you hook up your VCR to your computer."

"Right. For this, I found a scene that showed a raccoon down by the water, washing off a crayfish it had caught. Once I had it in the computer, I made a 3-D model of the raccoon in that position. Then I put the dimensions in to fit the one I had shot. Only, it was smaller because all I wanted to make was a form for the body." Tony paused, trying to figure out how to make his explanation understandable.

"So I got this model in the computer. Then a special program pretended like it sliced the model into little slivers, each a sixteenth of an inch thick."

"Like a meat slicer in the deli."

"Right. Then all I did was send the information, one slice at a time, to the cutter down in the basement. It cut each slice out of plastic sheets, and all I did was glue all of them together to make the real model. After that, I glued on the skin. Only it's a little more complicated. I mean you don't just throw on the skin, but that's most of it."

"I understand." Jarrod admired the taxidermy. "That's really great."

"We better get washed up. You can go first. Bathroom is over there."

Jarrod walked over and went into the bathroom, and began to wash his face and hands. Tony wandered around his room, looking at all his treasures. He loved learning about them, making them, and having them, but he loved it even more to be able to tell someone about them.

The hard part was finding anyone who would sit still long enough for an entire telling. That's why, during the summer when Tony really concentrated on his projects, his friends were pretty scarce. All of them loved the idea of a handmade crossbow but were only interested in how far, how fast, and how accurate it was. If it could nail a woodchuck at fifty yards, it was great, never mind what kind of glue held it together.

"All done," Jarrod said, coming back out.

"I'll just be a minute. If you want, go sit at the PC and watch my latest script. It's called 'Images of Death.' Just select it from the 'Movie' menu."

As Tony went to the bathroom, Jarrod sat down at the desk and began to operate the computer. In a few seconds, he was watching an original horror story. The images were animated, like cartoons, but pretty realistic. It was more like a moving comic book than a cartoon. The sound was great, too.

The main character, Dan Murphy, was a pretty odd fourteen-year-old who loved to do all sorts of weird projects, including making crossbows and blowguns the way they were made long ago. His weirdest project, though, was a special drill on the end of a long pipe. The bit was hollow, and had a light built into it. There was also a light tube, called a 'fiber-optic strand,' that ran up inside to the top of the pipe. In the top was a lens, so Dan could look through and see whatever the drill had drilled into.

The strangest thing Dan liked to do was go to a cemetery, drill down into buried coffins, and look at what was inside. One dark and spooky night, he drilled into a fresh coffin. When he was looking, he saw a strange creature come up through the bottom and begin to feed on the body. He had accidentally discovered a new kind of animal, a kind of cemetery mole that fed on human remains.

It wasn't an ordinary mole, though. It was bigger, much stronger, and looked mean. Dan was scared but didn't know what to do. If he pulled out the drill, the creature would surely notice. So he just stood there, almost paralyzed, and watched. It was gross watching a body being eaten, and Dan started to cry. Then, to his horror, the creature turned and looked straight up at him. Inside the tiny red eyes was evil.

Dan cried out and ran away from the fresh grave. But he only made it past a few rows of tombstones before the lawn under his feet started getting soft. All around, hundreds of the evil creatures were tunneling up to get him. Finally, the ground just gave way, and Dan Murphy fell in, never to be seen again.

"Pretty neat, huh, " Tony said, just about startling Jarrod out of the chair.

"Oh, wow, you scared me," Jarrod smiled, settling back down. "That's a great story. You must have just done it."

"Yeah, did it all yesterday. Why?"

"Oh, no reason. Great animation. It's surprising how much your mind fills in, once you get the scene going."

"That's why I figure a producer will see more of what I mean than by just reading words on paper."

"Shoot, you could even sell the cassettes directly. Put a dozen or so stories on one, have them duplicated, and sell them or rent them through a video store. You could be a producer."

"Man, I never thought of that. You think it's good enough?"

"For sure."

"I've got this other one I haven't done on the computer yet, but I've got the plot written out. Wanna hear it?" Jarrod nodded that he did, and Tony sat back down on the corner of his desk.

"Okay, there's this planet where this rich alien named Lamroo lives. He owns lots of mining planets, and is rich beyond belief. He has one of the biggest art collections in the universe. Lamroo's gallery is so big, it has entire wings. One of his favorite artists is a mind sculptor from Earth named Charlie Dirkson. He has a whole collection of his work.

"Charlie wasn't always a mind sculptor. He started out as a junk dealer, a salvage operator. One day, out on some asteroid, he found the remains of a crashed alien spaceship. Inside, he found this really strange machine, called a 'Titan Synthesizer'. It was something that hooked up to your brain and created whatever you were thinking about.

"At first, Charlie makes all the gold and diamonds he can. Tons of them, so he gets really rich, too. But then he gets bored. One day, just dinking around, he invents the first mind sculpture. What that is, is something ordinary that has been transformed by how he feels about it."

"Like making a milk carton look like a flower pot?"

"Sort of. Like he made this reproduction of a really neat spider from the planet Aysee. This spider was sort of kind, if you can believe that. If it ever caught a baby bug in its web or a female with eggs, it would let it go. So when Charlie Dirkson synthesized his sculpture, he gave his spider a heart of real gold. That kind of idea.

"Well, all that was really neat and all, and his ideas about things made him famous. But then he started getting a little carried away. Instead of just observing his subjects, he started capturing them. One time, he visited this planet and saw these little things named Pymites. They were like little crabs that scurried all over.

"Charlie wanted to do a mind sculpture of a Pymite, so he captured one and put it into a cage. All of a sudden, other Pymites from all over crawled out from the jungle and surrounded his spaceship. Charlie didn't worry, though, and just went on with his observing. But then the Pymite died. Just like that.

"Right away, from outside the ship, Charlie heard moaning. It was almost a wailing sound. The other Pymites were sad that the one had died. Then they got mad and started attacking the ship. Charlie couldn't take off in time, and they broke in and killed him.

"Years later, another salvage operator finds Charlie's ship in space. All the fuel is gone, and it's been drifting for years. Inside isn't Charlie Dirkson, but a mind sculpture of Charlie Dirkson, done by the Pymites. See, they were intelligent and hated him for killing one of their own, so they used his own machine on himself.

"The way Lamroo figures into all this is he ends up buying the last and most expensive Charlie Dirkson mind sculpture. The audience gets to see it the first time Lamroo sees it, and it's really gross. Because the Pymites hated him so much, the sculpture of Charlie is made up of the grossest things in the universe. Ah..." Tony became stuck.

"That's okay, but it's a little complicated."

"Yeah, I think I'll have to work on it some more. That's one of the good things about telling a story. If there's any rough spots, they really show up fast."

"I think it's about time to eat." Jarrod stood, but Tony hesitated. For just an instant, he showed a concerned, maybe sad look.

"What?"

"Oh, nothing. I just don't want you taking off like a bat out of hell because you think I'm weird."

"And talk too much? Don't worry."

"You think we can be friends?"

"Oh, yeah, I think it would be great. But…it might not be that easy."

Tony wasn't sure what Jarrod meant. Then, his mother called from the kitchen to let them know lunch was ready.

CHAPTER SEVEN

# The Runaway's Tour

Lunch consisted of cold fried chicken, potato salad, and soda. They sat outside, in the back, on the screened porch. It was a beautiful Saturday afternoon, not too hot like it sometimes got in the middle of July.

"So, Jarrod," Jill asked, "what do your parents do in Gates?"

"Ah, Mom and Dad have a small business. Yeah, they... they work in wood products. I mean they sell wood products. Burlwood and bunions for tables and stuff, and for making fiddles, guitars, banjos—sometimes even pianos."

Victor knew something about that, and said, "That's quite an art, knowing which part of a maple tree would make a good fiddle. You need to have a real, nice grain, but not too tight..." The man looked at the boy, giving him a chance to add more information. But Jarrod couldn't, and briefly looked away, out at the property. Then he looked back.

"Well, we really don't do that many fiddles—I mean wood for fiddles. Dashboards for cars. We do a lot of those. Did you know fancy cars—and even jets—use wood for inside?"

Tony came to his new friend's rescue by saying, "He thought my stuff was neat." His parents knew what he was doing, and went along with changing the topic.

"That's good," Victor said, taking another bite from a chicken leg. He chewed a little, and continued, "Did you get to try out his nest?"

"Nest?"

"That was the rope thing with the blankets hanging up in the corner. It's my other bed."

"Oh. Yeah, I saw it, but didn't try it. It looks great."

Jill smiled, "If Tony had his way, he'd have a room carved out on the top of a cliff in the Jurassic Period, so he could look down and watch the dinosaurs walk by."

"I think it's okay," Tony said, looking first at Jarrod, then at his parents.

"Okay?"

"That's our inside-talk that means Tony thinks you can have fun around here," Victor explained. "See, his room is just a warm-up. If you get through that, you'll really like the shop."

"Oh, yeah. I told him, I love stuff like that. I don't think it's weird; I think it's fun—like you do. Tony's lucky."

"So hurry up and eat so you can meet Ophelia," Tony urged.

Pretty soon afterward, the boys finished their lunch and headed over to the shop. On the way, they stopped at the bug cage.

"See the automatic fly catcher?" Tony asked, pointing to the special tubelike apparatus on the bottom.

"Yeah." Jarrod's voice trailed off as he touched the cage. It was beautifully made of black walnut wood and stainless steel. "It's really nice to see something and finally get a chance to touch it for real," he continued softly, mostly to himself.

"What?"

"Oh. Nothing. Just mumbling. That's a nice finish."

"We pressure-treated the wood with a non-toxic preservative and water-proofing. The cage wire and screws are all stainless steel. This should last outside for a hundred years."

"Why do you do things like this? Why is it fun?"

"Because it's the best something like this can be done. If someone who didn't know us only saw this bug cage, and looked at it really close, they would know us."

Jarrod kept gentle contact with the cage as he watched the largest mantis prepare to strike. A large black fly had landed a few inches from it. At first, the predator was still. Then, when a gentle wind moved through the cage, it began to move in slow, back-and-forth rocking motions. With each motion, it moved a bit closer. The wind stopped and the bug stopped.

"Kind of exciting, huh?" Tony whispered. The wind moved again, and so did the mantis, until it was right beside the unsuspecting fly. There was a pause—and then the predator struck, grabbing out with its spined forearms faster than the fly could escape. There was much buzzing and struggling. The four-inch-long hunter deftly repositioned the prey and made its first bites right behind the head. A few instants later, the struggling stopped.

"Neat," Jarrod marveled, finally moving his hand off the cage.

"Yeah, they're fun. I have spiders too, but I think these are the best to watch. Speaking of spiders, come on." Tony led the way to the shop.

"It's not really a big secret. My parents did projects ever since I can remember, but we really didn't get into the more expensive ones until about three years ago. That's when my mom inherited some money. Now, we're starting to earn some money on our own, so it should even out."

"Wow," was all Jarrod could say when they entered the large shop. Aside from The Horror Box, there were several other smaller projects in various stages of development.

"We're just getting into amusements, like I started to say before. This one...well, we don't have a name for it yet." They stopped in front of what looked like a ten-foot-long model of a pirate ship. On the bow was an ice cream freezer. In the middle was a four-foot-long glass cannon. Toward the stern was a very low sail.

"It's supposed to be an ice cream vendor's thing. Only the vendor would be dressed up like a pirate, and he'd sell ice cream cones and other things with a special topping. The topping is toasted amaranth. It's like miniature popcorn. The gimmick part is he'd pop the seeds right here, inside the cannon. It's high-tech too, so people should love to watch it." Tony pointed to the various components as he continued his explanation.

"You start out by loading in some seed into the cannon. Then you close off the front, so it's sealed. Then you shine in a beam from this laser, which raises the temperature of the seed up to where it would pop. But it doesn't pop because it's under pressure. Then the pirate pulls this and opens the front. All the seeds pop at once and the cannon fires—right into this sail, which catches it. Then it slides down here so he can scoop it up."

"Amaranth. That's what the Peruvians call *cueecha* or *sangorache*. It's one of the most nutritious grains known. You can eat the leaves and the grain."

"How'd you ever know that?"

"Read a lot, like you."

"Dad says we can even have little cards with an explanation of what amaranth is."

"One thing you probably would want to leave out is how the Aztecs used to make ceremonial figurines out of the seeds, glued together with human blood. When the Spaniards conquered them, they wanted to stop all their religious ceremonies. So they made growing amaranth illegal. If the soldiers caught an Aztec farmer growing it, they would cut off his hands."

"Man, you're an expert." Tony paused, thinking about it all. "You know, gross as it is, it's interesting. It might be something we could add to our little information card. Huh. Anyway, if you think of a name for it, let me know." The boys went to the next work area.

"This would be for someone who wants to have a mask of himself made. It's like those computer pictures, only in three dimensions. You sit here, let the video camera take your picture, and then wait about three minutes." Tony reached over and opened the lid of a suitcase-sized wooden box.

"This is the real invention part. This bottom is all little pins. They're flat now, but they move up and down to form a mold of your face. Then we put in a sheet of rubbery plastic that's been printed to look like your face, close the lid, and let it be molded to your shape." Tony picked up one of the test masks, which looked just like his father.

"You can give them out to your friends on Halloween," the proud inventor finished.

"If these things catch on—and I think they should—you guys are gonna be rich."

"That's what we hope. Anyway, this is our big one." They stepped over to in front of The Horror Box.

"This must be the famous. Horror Box."

"Right. Up there, up these creaking steps, is where Ophelia lives. I think she'd like to meet you. But first, I'll show you how the light board works. Just stay here." Tony hurried up into the trailer and began to operate the computer which controlled the front display of the amusement. The giant spider web came to life.

Even though Jarrod had seen it all before, it was like he was seeing it for the first time. Reality was so much more intense than watching that it almost brought tears to his eyes.

Being in the outside world was wonderful and terrifying at the same time, and he had to fight between seeing more or running away.

After the light display finished, Tony led Jarrod up to the wooden box, put him inside, and went back down to operate the controls. His meeting with the evil, venomous, screeching beast named Ophelia was something he would not soon forget. Even though he knew it was all pretend, there were moments when he was just as afraid as he was of his own dark things.

The two laughed for a long time after the demonstration ended, especially when Tony joked that Ophelia had been modeled after one of his teachers. Then it was time for Jarrod to go. They walked to the back of the shop and went out the door.

"Will you come back?" Tony asked.

"Sure. Maybe even tomorrow if it's okay."

"You bet." There was a short pause. "Hey, do you want to stay for dinner?"

"No, I can't. Not tonight. I better go."

"Okay."

"Thanks a lot, Tony. It was good meeting you. See you tomorrow." Jarrod started out past the gardens to the back of the property, toward the railroad tracks and his camp. Tony watched him for a few minutes, then turned and went back into the shop.

"So, what do you make of Jarrod?" Victor asked later, as soon as dinner started.

"I thought he seemed like a very nice young man. Very intelligent and polite. And he seemed to fit in with...us. Tony, you spent most of the day with him?"

"Yeah, I thought he was cool." The boy paused, looked down, and pushed around his broccoli a little.

"Go on, Tony, you can talk to us," Victor encouraged.

"Well, I like him, and I want him to come back. But I think there's something wrong."

"You mean that he ran away from home?" Jill asked.

"Yeah. He shouldn't just be there. I didn't really believe him about his parents."

Victor said, "Although he seemed to know about wood burls and...what?"

"He called them bunions," Jill helped. "We could always call information and see if there's a listing for Blackwell in Gates."

"But that would be spying on him."

"Not really, Tony. It might be doing him a favor. If I were his father, I'd want to know where he was."

"But maybe his father beat him or something."

"Your father's right, Tony. And even if Jarrod's father or parents were bad, maybe we could help. The first step would be to check."

"I suppose." The twelve year old took a small nibble of leg of lamb and mashed potatoes.

"Tell you what, let me just try something. Be back in a minute." Victor wiped his mouth, stood, and left the table. The two watched as he left the dining room and went into the living room. In a few seconds, they heard him pick up the phone, dial, and start talking to an operator.

Victor was on the phone for about five minutes, before he thanked the operator, hung up, and sat back down at the kitchen table.

"Afraid there's no record of a Blackwell in Gates or anywhere else around there. Not even in Salem. So if

Jarrod's a runaway, he's pretty far from home. If that's even his real name."

"He might have come down the tracks. You know, by hitching a ride on a freight train."

"It would be hard for him to get off here," Tony said. "There's nothing for them to slow down for. They go too fast to jump off." There was a long silence as the three continued to eat dinner.

"I don't know how far we should go into this," Victor started. "I mean I think we agree he's probably in some kind of trouble. A twelve year old just doesn't go camping out alone, not these days. Plus make up a story about who he is. I don't think it's interfering in a bad way to check it out."

"How?" Tony asked.

"Well, if he was in grade school anywhere, he would have been fingerprinted as part of the National Schoolage Identification Program."

"You mean get his fingerprints? No, I don't think that's a good idea. If it were me, I'd be really mad. He didn't ask for our help."

"He was hungry, Tony. You saw that much. And he may not have asked for our help, even if he needed it. Boys are just like that. I think that's a good idea, Victor."

Tony thought for a long time, and finally decided his parents were right. He hated the idea of spying on his new friend, but wanted to help if he were in some kind of trouble. Even if he had run away, it might be better to help him get home. Tony remembered when he thought of running away, and things weren't really as bad as they seemed. In the end, he was glad he hadn't done it.

"Okay, we can do it. But if it turns out okay, we shouldn't tell Jarrod anything. I don't want him to hate me."

Jill reached out and gave her son a comforting pat on his shoulder.

"I'll give Ed a call. All we need now are some finger prints."

"I'll get them," Tony volunteered. "He touched lots of things. Ah, I think I'm done." Tony looked at his father, who nodded it was okay for him to leave the table.

Tony went to his room, took the crossbow off the wall, and set it on his bed. It only took him a few minutes of rummaging around in his supply cabinet to find real police fingerprint powder and a brush. In a short while, he had found an almost perfect thumb print, which is all that would be needed.

After transferring the thumb print to a strip of clear tape, Tony stuck it on a piece of paper and ran the paper through the document scanner attached to his computer. Then he enlarged the print and used an image-processing program to enhance some of the details that were almost too faint to see. Finally, he got it ready to transmit to his uncle's computer at the police station.

Victor was just in the nick of time, catching his brother at home. Normally, Detective Magellan spent his entire weekend away from his apartment. He fished, hunted, skied, climbed mountains, jumped out of planes—did just about anything that was fun and full of action. Ed gave his brother the password to his computer at the police station, so they could start their search.

At six-thirty that evening, the thumb print of Jarrod Blackwell went into the National Schoolage Identification Program. If he had been in grade school anywhere in the country during the last eight years, it was just about guaranteed that a match would be found.

The three decided to check back with Ed's computer in about an hour. When they did, they were surprised to learn that no match had been found. They were even more surprised to see that the search had automatically been expanded to include the FBI Master File.

As far as they were concerned, the search was over. The FBI's Master File contained hundreds of millions of fingerprint records, but not of school children. It would have been nice to save time by cancelling the search, but Ed had gone out right after Victor's first phone call. They could have asked someone at the station to track him down, but that would have been making too big a deal out of it.

So the Magellans decided to call it a day and relax for the rest of the evening. Relaxing to Victor and Jill meant going out on the town—so Jill could strut her new, very expensive dress. They offered to give Tony a ride into town, but he declined, preferring instead to mess around at home.

CHAPTER EIGHT

# The Root

There were few things Tony liked more than a quiet summer evening in the garden. The corn was close to four feet tall, the potatoes had become bushes, the beans were almost ready to pick, and the tomatoes were ripening faster than they could be eaten. Even their giant pumpkin plants were starting to flower. Last year, their biggest pumpkin was nearly three hundred pounds.

Tony began to weed between the rows of corn, leisurely pulling out small tangles of purslane and crabgrass. The rich, musty smell of the soft dark soil was so thick he could almost taste it when he exhaled. It was a great time to think about nothing in particular and get ideas for new projects.

"Hi," Jarrod said then. Tony jumped a little in surprise. "Sorry, didn't mean to startle you."

"Oh, that's okay. Hi." Tony stood and brushed off his hands. "I was just sort of daydreaming." The twelve year old felt an immediate rush of guilt as he thought about checking up on Jarrod. "So, see you cleaned your clothes."

"Yeah." The visitor was a little nervous and kept looking intensely, like he wanted to say something but was afraid.

"The bats should be out soon."

"Tony, I want to tell you some things."

"Like you ran away?"

"No, nothing so...ordinary as that." They paused when a gentle breeze rustled the corn leaves all around them.

"I like that sound."

"Me too. You wanna walk?"

"God, this sounds serious. Sure. We can go down to the pond." The two left the garden and started out across the field.

"Should you tell your folks?"

"No, they're gone. Probably won't be back till midnight. So..."

"I guess the best way is to just tell you then show you. You'll think I'm nuts at first, and then you'll probably get scared, but then I think you'll like it." As they continued along, Jarrod tried to think of the best way to begin.

"I'm kind of like an alien."

"Oh, God, he's crazy," Tony laughed. "Sorry."

"I'm a hundred and forty-one years old, and I live in a great big hole underground." They stopped, Tony with a really concerned look on his face. He figured his new friend had escaped from the State Hospital. All in the same breath, the other boy finished, "I can create things out of nothing, and I fly around in a spaceship."

"But other than all of that, you're just a regular kid, right?"

"Hang on for just a few more seconds." Jarrod looked around and stepped over to several gopher mounds. He squatted down and began to smooth the mounds flat.

"And when there's a full moon, you turn into a gopher."

Jarrod laughed, "That might be fun to try sometime. Okay, you came this way, right? I couldn't have known we were going to walk this way. There's nothing under here except probably some pretty ticked-off gophers." Tony stayed where he was as Jarrod began to slowly sift his hands through the soil. It was fairly loose and crumbly, so was easy to do.

During the next minute, Jarrod imagined and dreamed of what he would create. He held his breath as the distant speck of light in the vast darkness suddenly expanded to something easily as large as the sun, filled with images of what was soon to be. The boy opened his eyes, exhaled, and smiled.

"This is for you." Carefully, Jarrod lifted what looked like a framed picture out of the loose soil. He shook it, puffed on it, and gently brushed it clean. "It's like a treasure map." The boy stepped back and held it out. Tony was reluctant at first, but then accepted it.

"The frame is black walnut, pressure-treated and water-proofed. It's one piece, too. No seams or joints. Look at how the grain runs. That's an aerial picture of about a few thousand square miles around here. Lower right is this place, and upper left is my place."

Inside the beautiful wooden frame was what appeared to be an aerial photograph of extraordinary detail. The inset in the lower right corner showed a much closer view of the Magellan's property, and the one in the upper left showed a close view of a very large Douglas fir tree.

"If you look real close, you'll see us standing right here."

Tony held the two-square-foot picture up to his face and squinted as hard as he could. Barely visible in the lower right inset were two specks that looked like the two of them as they would appear to someone in a passing plane. He lowered the picture and stared at Jarrod in disbelief.

"If you had a magnifying glass, you'd be able to see even more detail. If you looked at it through a powerful enough microscope, you could see individual blades of grass. If you kept on going, you could see pollen grains in the seeds on the blades of grass. It's infinite in detail and right in your hand."

"I'm listening," is about all Tony could think of saying. Jarrod leaned over and looked at the map he had just created.

"Let's see. Okay, the pond is down this way." The two slowly continued on their walk. "My dad and I were magicians. Our act was for me to make things appear, plus some other stuff. Dad said I was just born a few hundred, maybe a few thousand years early.

"In 1867, about this time of year, we were on our way to the Opal Creek Mine—which is still there, by the way—when we were ambushed by some Confederate deserters. Dad was killed. I got away by creating an escape tunnel. It didn't go very far. I was pretty sad, so I just stayed there. I made rocks that glowed so I could see, I made food, I made this thing that made air." Jarrod stopped and gestured as he tried to explain.

"It's hard to explain. Sometimes, I don't even know what I'm going to make. I mean I know what it will do, but I don't always know what it will look like. All I knew was I needed to breathe. So when I made something to do that, out came this thing that looked like a green rug." They continued walking, and soon could see the pond in the distance. It was starting to get dark, and bats were flitting around everywhere.

"After awhile, I just decided to stay there. The year 1867 was no time to be an orphan, let me tell you. Pretty soon, I just got used to it. I figured I'd wait until I was grown up and then go back up. I added rooms to the tunnel and pretty soon I had a pretty neat cave.

"To see what was going on outside, I made a crystal ball. Really. And it worked. I mean, I was a magician and a crystal ball is magical, so I just imagined one that I could look at and see the outside. It worked.

"I even made books to read. A lot of Jules Verne. That's what gave me the idea for a real place to live. One day, I decided to make a machine that could make things bigger than I could. See, I can only make pretty small things. That first tunnel, it was only about twenty feet long.

"Anyway, I made a machine to make me a bigger place to live. When I tried to dig it out, I laughed. It was about as big as a refrigerator and made out of this green crystal stuff. It probably weighed ten tons." Jarrod stopped again, so he could gesture and emphasize what he was saying.

"This thing ate rocks and grew bigger every day. It wasn't making me a place to live in—*it* was the place I was going to live in." They continued, slowly getting closer to the pond.

"Pretty soon, it was eating tons of rocks and dirt every day. It grew like a plant but was harder than a rock. It spread out and up and down. The bigger it got, the faster it got. In about two months, I had a room twenty feet high and about three hundred feet around.

"I almost went deaf. It was quiet as far as rock-eating machines go, but to be right there in it...wow. So, when I had that great big room, I thought that was it. But then this hole opened up in the middle. It got bigger as the sides got deeper, and it started to be like a mine shaft. I had to be careful not to fall in.

"Then the edge formed, so I couldn't accidentally fall in, and then the spirals. I named it the Root because that's what it reminded me of. A giant green crystal root." Jarrod paused, to catch his breath and think about how it all must sound.

"So when did it stop?"

"It hasn't. I think it's gonna go on forever. It's about thirty miles deep now and still going."

"Thirty miles? Straight down? It can't."

"It does."

"There'd be too much heat and pressure." Jarrod stopped again and laughed. "What?"

"Oh, you're right. That's why I'm here, in fact. There is almost too much heat and pressure. Right now, the Root's kind of struggling on how to adjust to it. It's still getting deeper, but sometimes it has to put all of its energy into just the very bottom. Everything else blinks out. That's why I'm sort of stranded here."

Tony looked at his map again, to remind himself that he was probably still sane, and that it was okay to be talking about giant green roots that were thirty miles long, built by a kid who said he was one hundred and forty-one years old.

"You know, if I find out I've gone nuts, I'll be really disappointed. This sounds like it could be fun, and I don't know if I'd want to come out of it."

"You're not nuts, believe me. In fact, you and your folks are some of the sanest people I know of. All you have to do is listen and see. Anything you think is nuts, there'll be a reason for. It's bizarre, but it will make sense." They continued walking and soon approached the water.

The pond was about three-quarters of an acre in size. Close to the shore was a huge old oak tree. Underneath the tree was a small wooden tombstone. The two boys stopped there.

The engraved words read, "LITTLE WHEATIE, ALIAS THE RODENT, FINALLY TUCKERED OUT. MUST HAVE BEEN ALL THAT PLAYING AND EATING AND BARKING. EVEN THOUGH SHE WORE US RAGGED, WE KIND OF, SORT OF, MAYBE MISS HER SOMETIMES." The engraved signature said, "HER LOVING SLAVES." Tears came to Tony's eyes, and he choked a little when he tried to talk.

"It's still a little hard to come here."

"I know. She was a good little kid. All she ever wanted to do was please you."

"You sound like you knew her."

"I did—sort of. The Root lets me see anything. I watched the day you got her." Jarrod stopped when Tony began to cry.

"Sorry," the boy said, turning to look out over the pond and the darkening sky. He took in a deep breath and his crying stopped.

"It's okay." There was a long pause. All kinds of frogs were beginning to croak and chirp from along the water's edge. Finally, Jarrod continued, "I think you weren't even two yet. It was really too young to get a puppy, and you were pretty rough on her sometimes."

"Yeah, kind of treated her like a stuffed toy."

"But she was tough. Do you remember when you tried to put her in that cardboard box?"

"And she bit me on the nose?" Tony began to cry and laugh at the same time. Tears streamed down his face. About a minute later, it was mostly laughing, and then it was okay. "Yeah, I miss that little creep. Ah, so your root's still growing, but it has blackouts."

"Yeah. I'm getting a little ahead. When it started to grow down, I decided to stay. I also decided to stay being a kid, like Peter Pan. I just used my hands, like I was taking a bath, and imagined I was still twelve." Without really thinking, Jarrod rubbed his right hand along his left arm, from his wrist up to his shoulder.

"Yeah, sometimes I think I don't want to grow up either. I think everybody thinks that." Tony slapped a mosquito as it landed on his forehead.

"The Root thinks or does something close to it. It understands what I say, even what I think, but it doesn't ever talk to me or anything. If I want something bigger than I can make, it will make it for me. That's how I got my ship."

"Your spaceship?"

"That's what it is, I swear. It's buried under the tent, or most of it is."

"That's why you didn't want me to look inside."

"Right."

"Did it break down? You said you were sort of stranded."

"When the Root blinks out, the ship loses power. They're linked together. It's working now, though. I came just to look around. I wanted to see Ophelia in person. I wasn't going to let anyone see me. That's how I usually do it. Then I got stranded and I decided to say 'Hi.'"

"Just like that?" Tony laughed a little, shaking his head in disbelief.

"Just like that. What I was thinking is you can go with me tonight. I'll show you around, and bring you back tomorrow."

"For real?" Jarrod nodded that he was serious. "And you're not nuts?" Jarrod shook his head that he was not and looked at the special photograph. "I guess I could leave them a note that I was going to camp out with you tonight. That would give me till morning...."

"Let's do it then."

"I don't know about this..."

CHAPTER NINE

# The Top of Tamarra

Tony put the wood-framed aerial photograph in his room, left a note for his parents on the kitchen table, and started off into the night with Jarrod.

"We really should have brought flashlights."

"What did I tell you? Trust me." As soon as they got outside, Jarrod crouched down in front of a flower bed and began to sift his hands through the loose soil. Less than a minute of creating later, he scooped away the dirt and revealed two walnut-sized, glowing marbles. He kept one and handed the other to Tony.

"Wow," Tony said.

"And they're just warming up." After a few seconds, each began to radiate with the intensity of a dozen car headlights. They were too bright to look at directly, yet only warm in their hands.

"I hope I'm not dreaming," Tony laughed as he and Jarrod started toward the distant campsite. Giant shadows played out around them as they held the glowing balls in different locations. Jarrod cupped his tightly within his fists to show the bones in his hands. Not to be outdone, Tony put his into his mouth. It looked as though he had half of a dark head, half of an orange one, with his teeth and jaw bone showing through from inside the orange half.

Wildlife seemed confused by the blinding apparition. Raccoons and skunks became nervous but still tried to keep on with whatever they were doing, while possums and deer just froze.

Soon, the two reached Jarrod's camp. Down at the railroad tracks, their lights reflected off the rails for as far as they could see in both directions.

"Now what?"

"Just toss them. I'll make them go away as soon as we chuck them." The boys threw the small spheres as far as they could and laughed at the spectacle created when they hit and bounced along on the ground. Almost immediately, the points of light began to dim. Soon, they were gone.

"Now for the real fun. Don't hurt yourself lifting." Jarrod positioned himself on one side of the tent. Tony followed his lead and got ready on the opposite side. Together, they lifted the tent upward and set it down several yards to one side.

Underneath was the top hatch of the ship. As soon as its owner touched it, it seemed to come to life. It was as if it were made of glass, and someone had turned on a bright green light inside.

"This is what the Root is made out of, too. Okay, get back. What I'll do is think that I want it up out of the ground." The boys stepped back, and the craft began to rise. A large amount of soil and rock heaved upward, then dropped away, as if being scraped off by an invisible hand.

The craft looked more like a big, flattened football than a flying saucer. It was close to ten feet long, five feet wide at the middle, and four feet tall. The green crystal hatch opened on the top.

"Climb in," Jarrod offered.

"You go first," Tony replied. Jarrod just smiled, grabbed hold of the rim of the hatchway, and swung himself upward to the top. He landed in a fully crouched position, then swung to a sitting position, and finally lowered himself feet-first through the opening.

"I'd say you have some practice. Okay, watch out. Here comes Old Leg Breaker." Jarrod ducked down out of the way as Tony prepared to copy his easy motions. Surprisingly, it all went smoothly. A few moments later, Tony was seated on the rim of the hatchway with his legs dangling inside.

"You gonna sit up there all night?"

"Sorry. It's my first time in a spaceship. I'm a little scared." Tony held his breath and slid down inside. Immediately, the hatch closed above him.

Inside the craft, Tony tried to be calm. There was absolutely nothing in there with them. No controls, no seat belts—nothing. The inside hollow was the same shape as the outside. The only feature was a small bench formed out of the crystal. Tony sat down next to Jarrod, in a very tight fit.

"Now what?"

"Now you just hold on and enjoy. Once we start, it's like this turns clear so we can see out all around us. Most of the time that doesn't really matter because we're going too fast to see anything anyway." Jarrod paused, trying to think of the right words to describe what was about to happen.

"I can't explain everything. Most of the time, I don't know how what I do works. Like I couldn't even start to explain how or why our lights worked. I just wanted them to, and they did. When I want to go somewhere, say right away, the Root just puts the ship over there. It's like the Root thinks me from here to there, and suddenly I'm there. It's too hard to explain. It's easier just to show you."

Jarrod gathered in a long breath, and continued, "I hope this doesn't blink out on us. Okay, all I do now is think I want us to go the Canary Islands, to my favorite spot. It should be real close to dawn there."

Tony could sense something starting to happen but wasn't sure what. There was a slight pressure difference he noticed in his ears, but no acceleration or movement. The green crystal shell of the craft seemed to blink a few times, changing from green to clear. When it was clear, he could see some points of light shining through from the outside.

"We're there."

"The Canary Islands? Aren't those near Africa?" Jarrod nodded that they were and stood up. The hatch opened above him, and he peered outside. Tony stood up too and joined him.

"Oh my God," Tony drawled in disbelief. They were on a grassy hilltop. It was dark and overcast, and there was moisture in the air. The warm smell of the tropical island seemed to ram deep into the boy's brain, creating an instant realization that he was far away from where he had been only seconds ago.

"We're invisible when we travel, even if we go really slow, and we don't ever show up on radar. There's never any wind drag either—it's like a corridor in the universe just opens up, and we slide through, not bumping into anything along the way."

The experienced traveler took in several deep breaths, enjoying the warm night. There were only a few lights visible in the distance, indicating they were out in the country of one of the islands.

"Show me if there's anyone around."

"What?"

"Oh, sorry. I was talking to the ship." Instantly, three-dimensional images appeared on the underside of the open hatch door, as though it were some kind of super radar. In the middle was a small image of their craft. Around them, at various distances, were other images. Most were of sleeping people, although one man was sitting. Only the people were visible, not the beds they were asleep in or the chair the man was sitting in.

"That's spooky," Tony whispered.

"That's okay, they're not close enough to hear us. That man will hear me in a second, though." Jarrod opened and closed his jaws a few times, and rubbed his mouth. "I'm learning Silbo. That's a whistling language they use around here. When they whistle, they can hear each other for two miles.

"I'm sort of a night phantom to them. Pretty soon, I'll have my own legend. Mostly, I say 'Hi' and tell them where to find lost sheep. Once I told them where to find a little boy who had gotten lost. Watch."

Jarrod took a deep breath, puckered his lips, and began to whistle. It wasn't ordinary whistling, though, but a purposeful pattern of bright, clear sounds.

"A canary in the Canary Islands," the boy joked when he paused to take in another deep breath. In a few seconds, the man who was seated looked up. Tony was amazed. It was as if they had a giant telescope that could look down from the sky at the man, and see through the roof of his house. Another person stirred, getting out of bed. It was a young girl who Tony knew, from her movement and posture, went to a window to look out.

"I just said hello, and that I have no news for them tonight, and that I hope they are all happy and well." Jarrod looked at the tiny image of the girl that seemed to be a few inches out from the bottom of the open hatch lid.

"That's Daria. Watch. She'll whistle back and ask me who I am." A few seconds later, wafting up from the valley below, came the questioning whistle of the young girl. There was a breeze, so the sounds drifted a bit, but it reached them in all its soft beauty. Jarrod whistled back.

"I told her that's my secret and that she should go back to sleep." A few seconds later, came another message from Daria. Jarrod laughed. "She says I'm dumb as a goat and probably smell like one." From the movement of the image, which was wearing long pajamas, they could tell Daria closed the window and returned to her bed.

The image of the man showed that he had gotten up and gone to a window as well. After a few seconds, from another direction, came his stronger whistle.

"That's Domingo. He never questions me. He just accepts. Once he thought I might be his dead son, but I told him I wasn't. Now he just listens and bids me safe travel." Jarrod paused to enjoy the unusual, anonymous friendship of the moment. Then he sighed and finished, "Speaking of travel, we've got a lot more to do."

Tony followed Jarrod back down into the craft. The images of the people faded, and the lid closed above them.

"Wait'll you see this next thing," Jarrod said, pausing to think his instructions to his craft. There was a change in pressure and some sense of change, but Tony could not actually tell they were moving.

All of a sudden, Tony became dizzy. The craft turned transparent, and he found himself looking down at the darkened earth from at least sixty miles in altitude. In the distance, he saw what would soon become a sunrise for Africa. It was like they were suspended at the edge of space with nothing holding them up.

Suddenly, they were moving—exactly alongside a basketball-sized meteorite. Tony knew that such things traveled at a few miles per second, yet he had no sensation of moving. As the object entered the upper fringes of the atmosphere, it began to glow. Orange changed to red, and that changed to white. The shell of the craft became tinted as the brightness increased, to protect their eyes.

Without warning, a fragment of the burning meteorite broke loose from the parent and hurtled—through them. Tony jumped and let out a cry of fright, but nothing happened. In an instant it was gone. They and their flying saucer could see the real world but were really not a part of it.

"This is the good part," Jarrod said excitedly as the main chunk of space debris began to vaporize. With a brilliant flash and huge burst, it was gone. Thousands of fragments, some no bigger than grains of sand, disbursed a few miles above the Earth.

"You're only the second person in the history of the Earth to see that happen. I'm the first. Okay, now where?" This time, the craft stayed clear. Tony watched as the stars above suddenly began to change direction as the direction of the craft changed. Although he felt no inertia, the sight was almost enough to make him faint.

"It's okay. It happened to me the first couple of times. You'll get used to it."

Before Tony could weakly say, "Okay," they were above a field of wheat near Stonehenge, in England.

"You're a pretty good artist. You should enjoy this." Slowly enough for Tony to follow its movements, the craft lowered and began to gently push over stalks of wheat. No sounds came through from the underside, but the twelve-year-old could imagine the soft scraping and brushing.

"Geeze, you're not...we're not..."

"Yup, we sure are. Tonight, we're going to do a pattern that looks Egyptian. The outer circle will be two hundred feet across, and have exactly thirteen sides. In the middle, we'll leave a smaller one, with the points where the sides come together pointed at the middle of the outer sides. That should get someone thinking."

"What if someone sees us?"

"They can't. There's no one around here anyway. The Root checks first, like it did in the Canary Islands. If there was someone in this field—or even close to it—we would have gone to another."

Tony began to laugh as the craft slowly completed its work. After another several minutes, they were done. Jarrod smiled, and then the craft settled to the ground. As it did, a small bundle of wheat stalks came right up through the bottom. It startled Tony.

"We're real now as far as this is concerned." To make his point, the boy broke several stalks. "They'll stay broken even after we go."

What happened next was enough to make Tony stand up as far as he could in the four-foot-tall confines and want to yell out again. The craft started to go under the ground. The wheat stalks turned ghostlike, seeming to halfway evaporate, and then rose upward as the craft sank. Ghostlike ground and rocks also passed through the interior space—and also through their bodies.

The motion stopped. Jarrod reached out and grabbed a ghost rock, which suddenly became real. He handed it to Tony, who slowly took it.

"Pretty neat way of mining, huh?"

"I'll say." Tony paused, set the rock down at their feet, then reached into his pocket and withdrew his wallet. From inside, he withdrew a library card.

"Salem Public Library, Salem, Oregon. Anthony Magellan, 77209 Highway 22, Salem, Oregon, 97301." Then the boy looked a little reassured, put the card back into his wallet, and put the wallet back into his pocket. When he saw Jarrod's confused look, he laughed.

"You can't read when you're dreaming. At least not the same thing twice and see it exactly the same way. For sure this is real."

"I told you." There was another change, and suddenly the ghostlike underground was gone. The rock remained, but the two were on their way to somewhere else.

A few seconds later, the craft arrived above Opal Creek Valley. It stopped alongside a giant Douglas fir tree, about three-fourths of the way up.

"This is Tamarra. It's an Indian name that means 'Father Spirit of the Forest.' It's almost eight hundred and fifty years old." The craft was clear again, so Tony could see outside.

Silently, the craft pushed in through the branches of the behemoth and stopped when its nose touched the upper trunk. Jarrod stood, and the hatch lid opened. Carefully, he stepped upward and out.

"Where you going?" Tony asked, standing to see where his friend had gone. Jarrod stood a few feet away, on a huge branch.

"You're next. Only be careful. Once we're outside the ship, we're just like regular people." He offered his hand to steady Tony, who slowly climbed out of the craft. As soon as he was safely on the branch, he sighed.

"Just don't look down. Even in the dark, it's scary to be over a hundred and thirty feet up. Here, hold on here." Tony let go of Jarrod's hand and immediately grabbed onto a smaller branch.

The craft changed back into glowing green crystal, then began to push in against the trunk. An opening appeared, into which the craft went. What was strange was the craft was much too large to fit inside. But it did anyway, seeming to flow into the opening a little at a time. Soon, it was all the way inside.

"After you," Jarrod gestured. Tony carefully let go, after making sure he had his balance, then slowly entered the opening. Jarrod followed. The boys actually climbed inside the tree, which was about four feet in diameter at that height. As if by magic, the opening grew smaller and smaller until it disappeared.

CHAPTER TEN

# Down Into the Root

"It's like it healed over," Tony said. The two were squeezed together on the inside of a green crystal cylinder. It was a bit under three feet in diameter, six feet tall, and made of the same perfectly smooth material as the craft.

"Now we're at a critical stage," Jarrod began seriously, a look of dread on his face. "There's something we both have to do in order to make it to the bottom alive."

"Geeze, I knew there was a catch somewhere. What?"

Slowly and carefully, Jarrod finished, "Don't fart." At first, Tony didn't even catch on that it was a joke. But then he did, and laughed.

"Okay, we're going to go down." Immediately, the floor started to drop away. It was fast enough to be fun but not so fast that it was scary. Whenever they touched or leaned against the wall of the shaft, there was no friction.

"Is this where our ship went?"

"Kind of. We're standing on it. The shaft is always here, and it's hollow. The ship forms itself into a cylinder—a plug—that goes up and down."

"Neat."

"I thought about a cave entrance, but people find caves. Plus this is more fun." The ride down lasted about a minute.

When they stopped, Jarrod warned, "This is another place to watch out. We're going to be up in the air for a few seconds, on top of this.

"I'm ready."

"Also, you might not want to look down. You'll be able to see down into the Root and it might make you dizzy."

"Okay."

The floor started to drop again, and then the shaft ended. There were no more smooth walls squeezing them together. Tony's hands began to sweat, and his mouth gaped open as a tumble of sights, sounds, and smells hit him all at once.

The safety of the elevator was gone. They were descending from up near the ceiling of a very large chamber, perched on an open surface not much bigger around than a garbage can lid. Everything was made of the same glowing greenish crystal. It smelled like a warm jungle, humid and a little sweet. The air was filled with bright tropical birds, which squawked and chirped and whistled.

Fifty feet down was the floor of the chamber. From their vantage, it looked like a giant donut. It was looking down into the donut hole that made the rest of Tony's body start to sweat.

The abyss was one hundred and fifty feet in diameter, with a bottom too far down to see. Cut into the walls of the abyss was a giant, unending spiral ledge that started at the top and went all the way down. The front of the ledge was a four-foot-high wall. Behind the wall was soil, and in the soil all sorts of plants were growing. There were even trees growing out from the spiral ledge, their branches reaching into the abyss. Some were so tall that their tops reached up to the ledge three turns up.

Less than a minute later, the crystal cylinder set down on the floor of the vast chamber. Even though he was still perched six feet up, Tony breathed a sigh of relief.

"Neat, huh? Okay, we're not safe yet. You stay there and let me get down, and then I'll be your spotter." Jarrod carefully sat down on the top edge of the cylinder, hung his legs over, and hopped off onto the floor. Then he stood ready to help as Tony did the same thing.

"This is it," Jarrod announced enthusiastically. He was instantly wound up and couldn't wait to start showing his secret world to his new friend. "Usually, it's night in here just like on the outside. There's still a glow, but it's really faint. It's boss too, what you'd call a 'magnitude seven,' when all the fruit bats come out. The reason it's..."

There was a sudden, loud cry from somewhere. Tony was startled and jumped a little. The strange noise had come from one of the large openings in the outer wall of the chamber. Jarrod smiled.

"That's Billy. Come on." The two went over to the closest opening, which was an open archway into Jarrod's bedroom. The place was unbelievable, like it belonged to some medieval prince who lived in a castle. Bright velvet tapestries hung everywhere, even over the bed. The bed itself was huge, with an enormous dark wooden frame.

Along the back wall were heavy wooden shelves, each holding many strange and fascinating objects. Tony had no idea what any of them were.

Jarrod went to his bed. On it, underneath the thick, beautifully embroidered comforter, was Billy. The lump he created was trembling in fear.

"Is that Billy?" Jarrod asked playfully. The lump trembled even more, and another sharp noise escaped. It was a combination of excitement and worry. "Whoa, is that our little Billy in there?" Jarrod laughed a little. "He wants to come out so bad to say 'Hi' to me, but he's afraid of you."

The lump jerked a few times, still trembling and came forward. The edge of the comforter slid back, revealing part of a small brown forehead and a dark eye.

"Is that the little Billy?" Jarrod encouraged in a happy, almost musical tone. Finally, his companion could stand it no more. Overcoming his intense shyness, the three-foot-tall creature emerged from underneath the cover and ran forward to hug Jarrod around the waist. There were more excited, happy sounds.

Billy was an alien, if ever Tony had seen one. He was chocolate brown in color, completely bald, and wrinkled all over. His shape was like that of a human, but his arms were so long his hands could easily touch the ground. The strange little being had large, dark eyes, no eyebrows or eyelids, a tiny nose, and no actual lips, only a circular opening for its mouth. Billy was wearing a tiny pair of shorts and a gold bracelet on his right wrist.

"Billy, I'd like you to meet Tony. Tony is my friend and will be visiting tonight." The tiny creature looked once, then let out a whimper, buried his face into his master's shirt, and tightened his hug.

"Billy's a little shy. He'll get used to you." Jarrod stepped back from the bed, his companion still clinging to his front. "That's my bat cave."

The bedroom was square, forty feet on each side. The back wall was solid green crystal. The front was solid too but had the opening to the outside. The two side walls were transparent. Behind the one Jarrod was referring to was a giant tropical tree. Hanging from every branch were huge fruit bats.

"Like I was saying, usually it's night now, and they're out flying around. There's thousands of other ones too, that don't come up this far. It probably won't be night again for ten hours. That's how the Root makes up daylight after it blinks out."

"What's in the other cave?" Tony motioned to the other transparent crystal wall.

"You'll see that later. Come on, Billy, let's show Tony the Root." Jarrod tried gently to pry his companion free, but it was too soon. The three went back outside into the main chamber.

"Actually, all of this is the Root, but usually we just call the hole part of it that."

On the way over, Tony looked up at the bottom of the elevator shaft, which was just a small hole in the ceiling high above them.

"What would have happened if the Root blinked out when we were on our way down...?" Tony's voice trailed off as other things occurred to him.

"Or when we were out chasing a shooting star?" Jarrod finished. Suddenly, his new friend looked a little pale. "It's okay. The Root would never let go of us while we were in danger, even if it meant it would get damaged. It would at least set us down first."

That seemed to reassure Tony, who switched his attention to the central abyss. With the utmost caution, he followed Jarrod and Billy to the four-foot-high wall. He hesitated—then looked straight down.

"Whoa," escaped from Tony's lips as he clamped both hands down on the top of the wall. Looking down into the Root was like nothing he had experienced before. It literally seemed to descend forever, an incredibly vast inside-out screw. Looking down at all the trees was like looking at a distant mountain. They got smaller and smaller until they looked like little dark specks of dust.

Tony had never seen so many tropical birds. There were flocks of them up top where they were, and also as far down as he could see. Way down, the center of the abyss seemed to be clogged with flying birds. There were also butterflies of every size and color flitting around among the birds.

"It's not like looking out of an airplane window," Tony finally said.

"No, it sure isn't. How you feeling?"

"Okay."

"As far as we can see is about fifteen miles, and it goes fifteen miles past that."

"And it's not red hot?"

"Nope. All the same temperature, all the same air pressure. Don't ask me how. We even have rain, right out from the underside of the spiral. Every other night, exactly half an inch."

"How come we can see colors if the light is green?"

"I don't know. I've never thought about it before."

Billy made some more noises then, much calmer than before. Carefully, he loosened his grip on his master and stepped down onto the floor.

"Hi, Billy," Tony said. The small creature glanced up for a second, then hugged Jarrod's leg.

"That's progress. Good boy, Billy."

"Where did he come from?"

"I made him. He's an imaginary playmate I had when I was real little. After a few years I got sort of lonesome, so I thought it would be nice."

"But he's...alive..."

"I know. Kind of scary, isn't it?" The two paused for several seconds. "Anyway, it's really neat when you get far down. See, there's always leaves and feathers, and dead birds and bugs falling. Sometimes, even whole branches. The hole is only so wide. After awhile, you'd have so much falling down the thing would get plugged up."

Jarrod paused, then bragged, "That's where the winds come in. Really powerful winds. They're like little dust devils—or leaf devils—that just hang out there in the middle collecting debris. The birds can still fly around them. When they get big enough, it's like there's a storm and all the stuff gets swept in onto the ledge at that level."

"Automatic mulching. Great idea."

"Just think, if there was no dirt and no plants, just all crystal, you could drop a marble here and it would start down that way and go around and around and around until it finally reached the bottom." Jarrod leaned out over the wall and pointed with his finger to illustrate the point. Billy let go of his leg, and began to make questioning sounds.

"Sure, you go ahead and pick dinner for all of us." Billy turned, slowly approached Tony, then cautiously reached out his right hand and touched above the human's left knee. Before Tony could touch back, Billy let out a little chirp of delight and scampered off down the ledge.

"He's going to pick some fruit and nuts for us. There's some ripening about five turns down."

"Great, I could use a little snack."

"Come on, I'll show you my room. Then you can meet the Dark Things. And then, if we're still alive, we can take a ride down in the hole."

"You mean down in that hole? Ah, sorry, Jarrod, I just remembered, I gotta get home now."

"Don't be chicken. You've lasted this far. You can do it."

"I'm not saying I will. But if I did, what, you mean go down in the ship?"

"We could, but that's not very exciting. I was thinking of the fun way." Jarrod started to walk down along the wall, the same way Billy had just gone. Tony followed. In a few minutes, they came to a large gasbag tethered to a tree.

The bag was like a miniature hot-air balloon, only much more ornate. The bag part appeared to be a thin leather ball, close to eight feet in diameter. It was painted with a beautiful scene of the Antarctic, showing icebergs and polar bears. A tasseled, golden net surrounded the bag. The bottom of the net attached to what looked like a parachute harness. Even the straps were decorated with bright designs.

"Oh no. If you think I'm going to strap myself into one of these things and jump over into that, you're nuts. No way, buddy."

"We'll see. I bet you'll change your mind. Come on."

The two headed back up to the top level of the spiral ledge. Near the top, which was sort of like the balcony, there were only small plants and grass. The woods didn't really start until the third turn down. It was pretty easy for Tony to relate it all to his own room, his own back yard, and the woods beyond. The reason he did that was because he needed to make as much sense of it as he could, so he could keep on absorbing it all.

"Don't be scared if you see one of our giant earthworms. Oh, and none of the bees has stingers."

"Did you pick the things that are in here, or was it the Root?"

"I did everything. There's nothing bad either. No poison ivy or anything like that. It's really kind of weird. I mean there were all kinds of bacteria in me when I came down from the outside, and there're probably all kinds in you. Some are good, and some are bad. The Root will leave us alone, but take care of anything we...deposit."

"Speaking of which, where's the bathroom?"

"In my room. But you can just go anywhere. Billy and I like to pee over the wall."

Maybe because he needed some relief, the remark struck Tony as particularly funny. The idea of this godlike kid who had been around for nearly a hundred and fifty years peeing off a ledge just hit him the right way. He began to laugh. Soon, they were back at the top.

"How come you seem like a regular kid?" Tony finally asked.

"Maybe because I am. It's funny, lifetimes are short. If you put a couple of them together, it's great and all that, but it's not magical or anything. I've seen a lot and learned a lot, but I've also forgotten a lot too. Mostly, I just keep going and have as much fun as I can."

"Huh, I thought you'd be this automatic wise man or something."

"I wish."

CHAPTER ELEVEN

# Jarrod's World

Jarrod led Tony over to the heavy wooden shelves along the back wall of his room. He stopped in front of one unusual object which consisted of an octagonal gold frame mounted on a gold base. It had what looked like a phonograph arm mounted on the rear of the base. The tip of the arm could barely make contact with the inside of the frame.

"This is our spider web game. Usually, we play it out in the dirt. When you tap the base, the arm starts to move. Anywhere the tip touches the frame, it attaches a strand of fake spider web. Then it draws it out until it touches somewhere else, and it keeps going until it makes a pattern. The pattern's never the same twice. The game is to try to guess what the pattern will be and be the first to draw it in the dirt."

The boy tapped the solid gold base, and the arm started to move. At the tip's first point of contact with the inside of the octagonal frame, it attached the beginning of an iridescent red strand. As the arm moved away, the strand elongated, attaching itself to the next point where the tip touched. Delicate ricochets kept the arm moving. It reminded Tony of a spirograph game he had when he was younger. Soon, a pattern began to emerge.

"And this one is just for daydreaming," Jarrod explained, stepping over to the next toy. It looked like a square sieve made of solid gold, one foot on each side and three inches thick. There were one hundred and forty-four holes formed into it, but they didn't go all the way through to the bottom. Jarrod lifted the toy out and set it down on the nearby wooden table.

The toy began to make a soft whirring noise. Suddenly, out of each of the holes came a half-inch shimmering whirligig. Each was a small pleated sphere, similar in appearance to a roof ventilator on a building, mounted on a tiny shaft.

The metallic bubbles rose into the air, slowly and gently dispersing around the room. Soon, they came alive with sparkling lights of every color. Anytime they touched one another or something else in the room, the soft rebounds caused changes in their light patterns as they headed off in new directions.

For the two, it was like being awake in a dream. The light and motion were so pleasantly distracting there was no way they could deliberately think of any one thing. Instead, their minds just wandered, thinking randomly about a lot of different things.

After a few minutes, the tiny floating spheres began to migrate back toward the toy, each homing in on the hole from which it came. Soon, the last rotating bubble settled in.

"Nice, huh?" Jarrod asked, picking up the toy and putting it back on the shelf.

"I'll say. Feels like I've taken a nap or something."

Jarrod had to struggle a bit to take down the next toy, since it was so heavy. It consisted of a two-foot square slab of green crystal, curved inward on the top. The boy took it to the table and carefully set it down on its side. Then he went back, picked up a stand which held five thick white candles, and set it down a few feet in front of the slab.

"This is one of the things we have in common." Jarrod rubbed the first candle wick between his right thumb and index finger. Immediately, it flared into life. Then he did the other four. The flames were exceptionally bright and seemed to penetrate deeply into the concave surface of the crystal slab.

"I make up stories too." The boy sat down sideways on the edge of the table and leaned over slightly so his hands were between the candles and the slab. They cast a dark shadow on the slab. At first, he kidded around, making little shadow figures.

"This is a dog, this is a flying bird, and this is an ostrich." Each time, he held his hands differently so that a shadow would appear on the slab. Then he began to concentrate and slowly churn his hands together. At first, they cast only their own shadows.

A few seconds later, Jarrod's hands began to change. Tony watched in amazement as they lost color and became translucent. He was actually able to see through them. Then sparkling lights started to appear inside the hands, similar to but not as bright as the lights inside the floating whirligigs.

"Wow," Tony said, looking at the slab. It was as if Jarrod's hands had become a projector lens. The bright light from the candles shined through and cast an image of what was inside of them onto the crystal. But it wasn't an ordinary image. It was in three dimensions and seemed to stand six inches out from the front of the concave surface.

"Once, in my old time, there was a town called Grady. Grady, Arizona. It was a mining town." An actual image of what Jarrod was describing appeared in front of the slab. It started with a full shot of the town then moved in until they could see the streets, changing just like the scenes of a movie. The boy would pause often, to give the pictures time to catch up to what he was saying.

"A group of Chinamen came in one day, on foot. They stayed by themselves and never spoke to anyone. Pretty soon, people in the town started giving them little odd jobs to do. The things they didn't want to do themselves."

Amazingly, the characters in the scenes started speaking to one another. All Jarrod did was describe what was happening, and the almost-living images seemed to take over by themselves. Tony almost lost his balance when one scene showed the local saloon. He could smell the cigars and the whiskey! The rising smoke didn't actually come out into Jarrod's room, but disappeared when it reached the outer edges of the scene.

Tony wanted to ask why the Chinamen looked like aliens and had blue skin, and why they never said a word to anyone in the town, but kept quiet so as not to interrupt the story.

"Every night, some of the Chinamen would walk outside of town and set up what looked like barber poles. Soon, the town started to be circled by these poles. No one knew what they were, and they couldn't ask because the Chinamen didn't speak. They just figured they were some kind of fireworks display for the Fourth of July, which was coming up, or for something religious.

"See, the problem was no one in Grady had ever seen a real person from China, so they didn't know they should be starting to get afraid. These were definitely not men from China. They were from outer space.

"One night, just as the last pole was being brought out, one of the miners decided he had to know what they were. So he confronted the group. He was mean, and he was a little drunk. When he yelled at them, their leader stopped and the others kept going with the pole.

"Of course, the Chinaman couldn't—or wouldn't—answer. So the miner tried to draw out his gun. Faster than he could, the alien bared his fangs, lunged at him, and took a big chunk out of his neck. It was gross. There was blood everywhere. People started to scream—and the Chinaman ran, faster than even a horse could run. The group made it to the outside of town and pushed in the last pole.

"Right away, there was lightning between all the poles. In a few seconds, the entire town was fenced in with energy. All the aliens gathered around on the outside. They were happy—and very hungry.

"What they had done was turn the whole town of Grady into a corral, like the humans would keep cattle in. Then it was time for the first feeding. Now this was gross. The leader went first. He stood up at the fence and opened his mouth and spit out a great big glob of green goop. It was like a lizard's tongue, only much more gross. The glob had fangs of its own and stayed attached to the alien's mouth by a strand of web. It was thinner than a hair, but much stronger than any steel.

"The glob flew into the town, bit the first person it saw, and just hung on. Then it started to retract back to the alien, being pulled by the strand. People tried to chop the strand with axes, but the axes split. When the sheriff shot it, it cut the bullet in two pieces and knocked out two separate windows in the building behind them. Pretty soon, the person couldn't fight anymore and fainted, which was probably a good thing since he didn't want to be awake when the aliens started feeding. And so the unconscious bodies were dragged out of town, through the energy fence—then devoured by the hungry aliens."

Jarrod didn't continue, and soon the last image faded away. He smiled. Tony was speechless. Jarrod began to concentrate again, and continued slowly churning his hands together.

"Sometimes, I don't even have to say all the details. If the setting is complete enough, the people and things will just go by themselves." The boy became silent again and continued to concentrate.

"This is one I just thought of, a few minutes ago. Once, there was this guy named Tom Ratson. He always got picked on when he was a kid. The other kids called him Tom the Rat, or Son of a Rat. Anyway, he grew up kind of tough—and weird. He was like a young version of Bruce Dern. He was a real loner too. Never had any friends. The only job he could ever find was working in a carnival.

"He got hired one day by this rich guy to operate a new amusement the guy had bought. The guy wanted the money from running it but didn't want to have to do the work. The ride was called The Horror Box and was the hottest new thing going. All the kids loved it."

Tony was instantly enthralled. There, in the three-dimensional images, was the Magellan's creation, as if their dreams for the future had come true.

"Most girls were afraid of Ophelia, and so they had to go with guys, who would protect them. Plus girls would never, never pick up the eyeball in the bowl of slime.

"Even though Ophelia was just a robot, Tom started to like her. She said things to him that weren't in her program. Maybe it was all in Tom's head, but he did hear her say these things."

In the scenes that followed, the character named Tom was cleaning up inside the box after the carnival had closed for the night. Ophelia, in her evil, raspy, hissing voice told him what a good person he was for taking such good care of her. She was still wicked through and through but kind toward her keeper.

"Ophelia became the first real friend Tom had ever had. As the days went by, he actually started to love her in a strange sort of way.

"That's when Jimmy Duroc came along. Now Jimmy was pretty maladjusted on his own. His nickname was Duroc Pig, and he looked and smelled like one. His only purpose in life was to make the lives of other people miserable.

"He'd already done a pretty good job on his parents. He was only ten years old, but his mom would do anything to keep him out of the house all day. That's why she loved it when the carnival came to town. Even though she had to go without food, she gave him all the money he needed to stay out all day and most of the night.

"When Jimmy saw Tom getting ready to open up The Horror Box one morning, he knew he was in for some fun. Tom was so puny, so weak, so vulnerable-looking. So Jimmy decided to make Tom's life miserable, by sabotaging Ophelia.

"Jimmy was too big to fit inside the box with anyone else, so he always went alone. His first time in, he left a big wad of bubble gum on Ophelia's face. The next time, he left a little bag of dog droppings in the box, so the next kids in would step on it.

"By then, Tom was in a near panic. From inside the trailer, he started checking after each ride. The third time Jimmy was in, Tom caught him with a can of spray paint, ready to really mess up Ophelia. So Tom threw him out and told him never to come back.

"Ophelia told Tom how hurt and angry she was. She wanted revenge. She also said that Jimmy would be back, probably in a disguise. Now how she knew that I'll never know, but she did. So she and Tom got ready. Tom changed her programming just a hair—and then they waited.

"Sure enough, Jimmy came back—disguised as a really big girl. Tom let him up there. But when he tried to use his can of spray paint, Ophelia jumped onto him and tore him apart.

"The kids down below thought the screaming was great. And the blood dripping out from the box—well that was great, too. And the extra-large web-wrapped body—or body parts—that dropped out next, hey, that was the ultimate. The kids went crazy. They even booed—but just in fun—at Tom when Tom closed the ride for a few minutes to go up and clean inside the box. Gosh, he needed a water hose.

"But then, the ride went on. The web-wrapped pieces got taken out with the rest of the carnival trash that night, and Jimmy's mother never saw him again. Funny, she never said anything to anyone, and no one ever said anything to her. I guess they were just glad he was gone."

The last scene was of Jimmy's mother, peacefully sitting at her kitchen table at home, enjoying a cup of hot chocolate. Jarrod smiled as the image faded.

"You are one sick dude," Tony laughed.

"Yeah, I kind of like gross stories."

"I think I can use that one for my project—if you'll let me."

"Sure, it's yours. Oh yeah, before I stop, they don't have to be made-up things. If I were to want to see what dinosaurs were like, all I'd have to do was think about how they must have been..." Jarrod's voice drifted off as he began to concentrate. His hands were still translucent, still filled with a galaxy of tiny lights. As he churned them together, an image of a prehistoric landscape formed.

The three-dimensional image showed a pack of tyrannosaurs stalking a pack of grazing plateosaurs. The meat-eaters were crouched down in the tall grass, their chests scraping against the ground. Tony had never seen them portrayed like that, and expected them to be upright.

"Go ahead and put your finger in close to them," Jarrod whispered.

Tony hesitated. As he leaned down close to the image, he could smell the tropical warmth of the ancient world. He could also smell the dinosaurs, something he could never describe. Then he put his right index finger into the scene, and moved it close to the first tyrannosaurus. Suddenly, the tiny image of the beast turned and snapped at him. Tony reflexively pulled away and let out a little noise of fear. Then he started to laugh.

"Shhhh. They're about to attack." The lead predator directed its concentration back toward its prey. It and the three others continued their down-low stalk until they were very close. There was a brief hesitation—and then the tyrannosaurs charged. The dozen or so plateosaurs began to flee. The predators selected the slowest one and converged on it. While one turned it, another tried to cut over to come in alongside of it.

Separated from the herd, the unfortunate plateosaurus was doomed. It stumbled—and then one tyrannosaurus was upon it. Soon, the other three caught up and began to feed. There was much screaming and growling and chomping. Soon, Jarrod pulled up his hands and the image faded. In a few seconds, his hands returned to their normal color.

"That was fantastic," Tony laughed.

"Thanks." Jarrod blew out the candles, then brought them and the holder back to the shelf. Tony helped by carrying back the green crystal slab.

"The thing about doing that is the images are authentic. What I mean is they come from inside of me, and I don't even know what they're supposed to be like. But they come out right."

"How do you know that?"

"Because they're the same as the Root would show me," Jarrod paused as he caught himself. "Oh yeah, I haven't shown you that yet. See, all I have to do is ask the Root to show me something, and it does. In any wall or ceiling—anywhere I'm looking." The two looked over at the front wall. Suddenly, all around the arched opening to the outside was a continuation of the dinosaur scenes. It was as if the entire surface were a reflection slab. The image was larger, and seemed to be just behind the surface, not out in front of it like it did with the slab. After a few seconds, it faded away.

"When the Root does something like that, it does it accurately. It's like a giant computer that knows everything. To construct an image of a dinosaur, it would find a fossil, look for an intact fossilized cell, and read the genetic code from the fossilized DNA. Then it would apply that code to an imaginary living thing, and come up with a dinosaur."

"Like Jurassic Park. Ever read that?"

"I was almost there as Mike was writing it. I mean I was there, but he didn't see me."

"Could the image have bitten me?"

"No. You would have felt a brush, but not a real bite." Jarrod turned then, and walked up the clear wall in front of the vast, dark cave.

"This is where the Dark Things live. They... " Billy chirped out then and came hurrying into the room. He barely made it to the bed before his collection of fruit dropped out of the folded leaf he was using as a bag. The small creature chattered in relief.

"Guess we'll eat first," Jarrod said.

CHAPTER TWELVE

# The Dark Things

Their snack consisted of freshly picked bananas, oranges, strawberries, and pecans. While Billy laid out the feast on the large quilted comforter, Jarrod went to get three glasses of water.

"Here, freshest water you've probably ever had." Tony took one glass, which was made out of green crystal, and took a sip.

"Yeah, great." Billy hopped up onto the bed, while the other two sat on the side. They set their glasses down on the floor, beside their feet.

"So, you believe it all?"

"Sure. I mean I'm here. It's kind of strange. It's so strange it seems okay. I mean like you said, even if it seems impossible, at least it makes sense."

"Whatever that means." They both laughed. Even Billy chirped in happiness, although he didn't understand what was funny. From outside the room came the loud squawks and chirps of the passing birds. Occasionally, a bird would come in, but then dart right back out. The butterflies and bees stayed in longer, but ended up heading back out into the brighter chamber above the vast abyss.

"So what's a Dark Thing?"

"Things. I have two of them. They're just monsters that live in the cave back there. They're big, about like a car, and really mean. All they want to do is kill me."

"Okay."

"No, really. See, I used to make them at night, to play with. I'd run out in the dark, get afraid of them chasing me, and pretty soon they'd be there. They were almost real, but not quite. I mean they could hurt you. Definitely tear you apart. But they're like big black ghosts, so they really can't control where they're going. If you jump down, they just keep on going. Dad and I used to play this game. I'd bring them, he'd throw a great big net over them, and we'd ride them up into the air."

"Wow."

"Yeah, it was great. Never got very far. As soon as I stopped being afraid, they'd start to dissolve, and we'd come back down. After all this grew, I started getting a little bored, so I made a few of them real. They're still like ghosts, but they don't go away when I stop thinking about them."

"And you just play with them?"

"Yup. I go in, they come after me, and I run away."

"Oh, so the Root would protect you if something went wrong?"

"No way. That's what makes it exciting. The Root can't—or doesn't—change what I make myself."

All of a sudden, Tony wasn't so anxious to finish his snack. But he did, and then went to use the bathroom. Instead of a toilet, there was a green crystal two-hole outhouse seat, one for Billy and one for Jarrod. And instead of a sink, there was just a green crystal counter, with an always-flowing stream of water coming out from the back and running down into a drain. There was toilet paper, the softest Tony had ever felt.

"There, all set."

"Great." Jarrod was getting excited again. He wiped his mouth with his hands and then his hands on his pants, and just about hopped over to the clear crystalline wall sealing off the cave. Billy made a whimpering noise and scurried down off the bed and outside.

"He's chicken when I stir up the dark things."

"Maybe I should take the hint."

"You'll be okay. You can run faster than me." Jarrod rubbed his hand across the wall, and a door suddenly slid open. Where there hadn't even been a seam a moment before was now an arched doorway.

"Yoo-hoo, we're here. Come and get us," Jarrod called into the gloomy distance. He boldly stepped through, but Tony hesitated. "Come on, they're usually way in the back." Reluctantly, Tony followed.

"This stays open?" Jarrod nodded that it did. "What if there's another blink-out?"

"I suppose the door would stay open. But blinks don't happen just all of a sudden. There's flickering and stuff, so you have time to get back out and close the door. The door will never close when you're inside."

The cave was large and craggy and damp. It also smelled, like what Tony imagined a graveyard would smell like if it were all dug up. Almost immediately, they heard the first distant moan. It drifted and echoed in the near darkness.

"That sounded like a person."

"They're just trying to trick us."

"They're smart?"

"Not really—just a little sneaky. We're smarter." Next came a pretty substantial squeal, clearly from something very large.

"Ah, must have smelled you. Different-smelling meat. Very exciting to them." The two continued deeper into the cave. Minutes seemed like hours, and Jarrod's room seemed to be miles in the distance.

Suddenly, there was a low-pitched but strong pushing sound. It was almost a scraping, as if two giant balloons had been rammed together.

"Blind attack!" Jarrod yelled.

Before Tony even understood what was happening, he was running in the opposite direction as fast as he could. Jarrod was right beside him. All he remembered seeing were two huge orange eyes suddenly open a few dozen yards away. They were full of hunger and hatred—and moving toward them at a very fast rate.

The dark things roared out in anger and increased the speed of their pursuit. They continued to bump and scrape into each other, and some of their hateful screams were at each other. Each wanted to be the first one to capture and devour the fleeing humans.

Tony ran as fast as he had ever gone, but the door still seemed too far away. There was more scraping and bellowing—and then they made it. Both boys hurtled through the door and made a flying crash down onto the bed. Tony was moving so fast he touched down in the middle and nearly bounced off onto the floor on the other side. Instantly, the clear crystalline door slid closed, trapping the dark things.

The two horrible creatures could not stop and struck the clear wall. With great screeches of displeasure, they rebounded. Tony and Jarrod picked themselves up and hurried back to watch.

"My God," was all Tony could say. Each monster was more than nine feet tall and six feet wide. They had no clearly defined legs, but did have two massive arms. On the end of each was a set of giant claws. The mouths were small caverns full of razor-sharp fangs. The eyes, each as big around as a large dinner plate, bulged and stretched. They were more a fiery red than orange, and the pupils were as dark as anything the boy had ever seen.

The two beasts roared out and slowly came to the wall. Together, they began to push. There was a frightening stretching sound, and the wall began to bulge outward.

"I'm outta here!" Tony called.

"No! Stay. They can't get through." Jarrod tried to catch his breath. "They're just testing it." Tony, gasping in air, stepped back anyway.

"What's a matter, poor babies?" Jarrod taunted, stepping right up to the wall. "Haven't eaten in a hundred years or so? Poor things. Better luck next time." The boy started to laugh. The Dark Things bellowed again—then began to retreat. They continued to look forward, slowly moving backward into the near darkness. Soon, their eyes closed, and they were gone.

Jarrod took one last really deep breath and said, "That was close. A blind attack is when they close their eyes, come out of hiding, and start coming. If they hadn't bumped into each other like that, they would have been even closer before we saw them. Then it would have been the wind they were pushing we would have felt. That would have been real close.

"Sometimes, they try a slow blind attack. But all you have to do with that is keep looking for a big area that's too dark. Like a giant shadow. Once they even tried an ambush. One was up on the ceiling, eyes up, so I couldn't see the shadow until I was almost underneath. The other one stayed way back and tried to make noises like they were both back there. Then the first one dropped down. It was great. Might have worked too, except it took forever to pick itself up and come after me after it hit the ground."

There was still nothing Tony could say. Jarrod stepped close and gave him a few firm pats on his right arm.

"You did swell. Good thing you can run fast." Finally, Tony smiled. The two boys returned to the bed and sat down to finish catching their breath.

Finally, Tony asked, "You said the Root could show you anything. Did you mean *anything?*" Jarrod paused before answering, a pretty serious look on his face.

"Yeah, but I think I've shown you enough for right now. See ..." For the first time, the ancient boy became stuck on words. "There's a lot that happens in the world, or has happened. If I wanted to see George Washington, the Root would do the same thing as with the dinosaurs. It would find his remains, copy the genetic pattern from one of the cells, then use that information to create a human image. Since Washington was long since gone before the Root ever came into existence, it can't recreate accurate historical things. But it could check all existing references to a certain event, then recreate it for me."

"How does it check?"

"With thought. That's as much as I've been able to figure out. If it exists and the Root can think of it, then it's here. What's ... I don't know, great or scary, depending on how you look at it, is it knows everything that happened after I made the first machine. Everything in history after that, it has a complete record of. All the wars, all the ..." Jarrod choked a little on his words, then became still. Tears welled up in his eyes.

"What?"

"When I was still learning how to use it, I asked to see things. It was sort of an accident. I didn't really know what I was asking." There was another long pause as the boy tried to figure out a less painful way to recall.

"What I'm trying to say is I've seen people killed. Lots of people killed." Jarrod's voice dropped off. Almost too faint for Tony to hear, and with a degree of shame, he finished, "tortured too." Then he wiped his eyes and sniffed.

"I still don't understand how we can be so mean to each other."

"We can sure be that."

"There was this movie once, about this alien invasion. Only it wasn't a bad invasion. At the end, only the bad people in the world died."

"I think I've seen it. An old black and white one."

"I thought about doing it. Really. Only my way was with hard flies. Little crystal sand flies with a poison bite. One for each bad person in the world. I thought about asking the Root to make them and let them go. There would have been millions of them."

"What happened?" Jarrod didn't answer the question right away.

"The way the Root was going to identify the bad people was to go out, with its thought power, and capture the thinking patterns of everyone on Earth. One at a time. If they were bad, they would have a hard fly created for them. If they were good, they were passed."

Sounding as if he were defending himself, the boy continued, "It wasn't as hard as I thought to identify them. It didn't matter how smart you were or how dumb. If you were cruel and could cause pain to someone else without caring, you were bad. Even some kids, some kids five years old, were bad. Just from their thinking, we knew they were cruel and would cause pain later on.

"What happened is I stopped. I couldn't do it. It wasn't right for me to kill people, even bad ones." Almost ashamed to admit his weakness, Jarrod turned to Tony. "There are people out there who can skin somebody alive, and I mean really do it with a knife, and I can't kill them.

"They deserve to die, Tony, they really do. They have no business here with the rest of us."

"That's okay, Jarrod. Just because you have this...this gift, doesn't mean you have to.... Besides, they'll get caught."

"That's another thing. I used to ..." Jarrod was too tired and stopped. They sat there for nearly a minute, a long time for kids who were supposed to be having fun.

"Sometimes it's not so easy hanging around all the time."

"I guess not."

Jarrod brightened and said, "Anyway, the Root can think a distance a little bigger than our solar system. That means it can think the ship to the planets."

"You're kidding."

"I'm the only human who has been to Saturn."

"No!" Jarrod nodded his head that it was true.

"What's even neater is...well, it's hard to describe. A telescope gathers light, right? If you get a big enough mirror, the photons coming in from a galaxy billions of lightyears away are just enough to give you a fuzzy picture. The Root can collect light from as wide around as it can think. So its mirror is as big as our solar system. It can show me pebbles on planets four billion light years from here."

"And..."

"Can't tell yet. The light that gets here is so old, it's way before any other life could have started. So I still don't know, even with the Root.

"One time, I thought I had it all figured out. I thought, maybe Heaven is the same for everyone, no matter how far away you live. So I thought all I'd have to do is ask to see it, and just look for the aliens walking around.

"Nothing. I know there's something there, but I haven't seen it yet. That's what's frustrating. If we're talking things, light photons, fossils, gene patterns, stars, brain waves, the Root can process them. But abstract things like death and what's out there—so far, zip. I think if I ever get to understand anything like that, I'll be able to teach it."

"Sounds just like a dumb old computer. Oh, amazing and all that, but just a dumb old machine."

"Or else it's really smart, and it doesn't think I'm ready to see."

"That would be interesting."

Jarrod stood and said, "Come on, let's go somewhere. You're not tired yet, are you?"

"Are you kidding?"

"Good. First, I'll make you a gasbag. They're really fun. Then we'll take off again. I've got some things in the Amazon Jungle I've been wanting to take care of. Then we'll go back to your place and get some sleep."

"I guess if I lived through the dark things, the rest is easy."

"Right." Anxiously, Jarrod led the way out of the room. Not too reluctantly this time, Tony followed.

## CHAPTER THIRTEEN

# Lighter than Air

"My folks would really love this. You think they could ever see?"

"Maybe. They *are* grown-ups."

"But they're good ones. They're really just like big kids. Really, that's what they call it, playing grown-up, whenever they get regular jobs or go out to show one of our things."

"Yeah, they are pretty neat. I think we can trust them. Let's just see what happens." They walked slowly, as close to the four-foot-high wall as the plants and trees would let them. The slope along the spiral was just steep enough so they could tell it was downhill.

"What's the dumbest thing you ever did?" Jarrod liked the question and smiled before answering.

"Probably one time when I went into this saloon to eat with my dad. There was a girl there, I mean ... " Jarrod motioned with his hands up around his chest. "I just stared at her. She saw me and said something about tiger's milk, and everybody started laughing at me. What about you?"

"There's too many to pick just one. Mostly, I say stupid things. Like I should just not say anything, but I go ahead and say something. Once, my mom and I met the Governor. He shook my hand, and it was all cold and sweaty. Instead of just saying, 'Hi, Governor,' I said something like it must have been raining outside. What raining outside had to do with my sweaty hand or meeting him I'll never know—plus it was the middle of July, and it was dry as a bone outside." Tony still cringed at the recollection.

"Oh yeah, and once I tried to make a shrunken head. I got this bright idea that all I'd have to do was make a clay mold of my head, let it dry and shrink, and then make a mold of it, and keep on going until it was small. It started out okay, but the clay didn't really shrink that much between times. I was too dumb just to give up, so I kept on going. It took thirty-one times before it got down small enough. By then, I hated it. And it didn't even really look like me by then, either. It was just a total waste."

"I think I remember that," Jarrod said, pausing briefly to look around. All of a sudden, images of a younger Tony appeared on the inside face of the crystalline wall. They stopped to watch as the ten-year-old plucked out strands of his own hair to imbed in the soft clay scalp of his model shrunken head. The images appeared just behind the surface, in three dimensions, and had sound. After watching for a minute, Tony began to laugh. Then the images faded.

"That is so amazing." The two started walking again.

"I'm a watcher. It's like I have friends all over the world. I watch people being born, become kids, grow up, and grow old."

"How do you even find them?"

"I don't. The Root does. It knows what I like and searches all the time. That's how it found you. Actually, it found your dad first, when he was just a kid. He was pretty weird."

"I'd like to see sometime."

"Sure." The two kept going and soon reached the spot where the gasbag was tethered to the tree. Billy chirped from behind some bushes and came out to join them.

"There you are, you little chicken." The small being came over and hugged his creator. "Everything's okay. Good boy."

Jarrod crouched down and began to smooth his hands through the soft humus. It was so rich it was almost black in color, and gave off a thick, sweet, musty smell when disturbed. The boy closed his eyes, tilted his head back, and began one of his creation dreams. Seconds later, a small mound began to rise up underneath his hands. He opened his eyes, took in a deep breath, and started to dig out his latest creation.

Billy and Tony squatted down and began to help. Soon, they uncovered the top of a flattened gasbag. The more they exposed, the more amazed Tony became. The bag was a leatherlike material, richly painted with a scene from the boy's life. It showed him inside the Horror Box, face to face with Ophelia. The painting was stylized, not a photograph, and could have been done by Norman Rockwell himself.

"That's great," Tony said. They all grabbed hold and stood up, lifting the deflated bag and harness out of the ground. Jarrod led the way to the wall, draped over the harness, then tied it to the closest tree branch.

"Now we just wait," Jarrod said, watching the bag. Almost on cue, it began to inflate. "If you'll help ..." He grabbed the bag again and started to push his end up over the top of the wall. Tony assisted with the other half. Billy also tried to help but was really too short. Finally, they pushed it over the wall and into the abyss. It hung straight down, continuing to inflate.

Jarrod smoothed out the soil they had disturbed, replacing the few small plants they had uprooted, then sat down facing the wall. Billy sat next to him.

"It'll be a little while. Sit." Tony did, and Jarrod continued, "This is a few days ago, at the Clubhouse Square in Lexington, Mississippi." An image of an old man appeared on the wall. "That's Lucious. He's ninety-two. One of the best jazz singers around."

Lucious began his performance, singing in a voice that seemed even older and raspier than he was. It wasn't singing in the regular way, but kind of talking with a rough melody. There was depth to the song, from years of hardship and hope. Tony imagined gazing down into a calm, slightly dark pool of water over ninety years deep. After just a few minutes, he almost knew what it was like to be the son of a southern slave.

The old man continued his song with a fife, the sharp, bright notes going back to lay on top of the words he had already sung. It was as though they could hear the two together, as if there had been a second Lucious playing the fife at the same time the first was singing. It wasn't hearing the words over from memory, though, but rather still having their feeling left over. Soon, Lucious finished, and the image faded.

"Pretty neat, huh?" Jarrod said a few seconds later.

"I'll say. I've never listened like that before."

"See what you've been missing?"

Tony was surprised when he looked up and saw the second gas bag floating in the abyss. He wasn't even sure how many minutes had gone by. All he did know was it was time to get scared. His palms began to sweat and his adrenaline pump. He looked at Jarrod, who smiled.

"Let's do it," Tony said, nearly springing to his feet.

"That's good, Tony," Jarrod laughed. "If you pretend you're not afraid, it might help."

"Afraid. Hah! No problem."

Jarrod stood too, brushed himself off, and went to the wall. He reached out and tugged on the new gasbag, and was pleased at how much resistance there was. Then he stepped down to his own, pulled in the harness part of it, and strapped himself in. After tugging on the various straps to make sure they were tight, he sat up on the top of the wall, his back toward the abyss. Without a word, Tony started to do the same with his own harness.

"It's pretty neat, Lucious made his fife like you made your blowgun. He used a piece of Mississippi River cane, burned the holes in with a hot poker, and burned the hole all the way through too."

"Oh," Tony said, pretending that he was interested. He was actually afraid of dying, and that's all he could think of. In a way, Jarrod was having fun with him.

"Yeah, and it's kind of funny, but before he burned the holes in, he licked each spot to make it wet. I wonder if that was so it didn't start to burn, just smoke."

"Maybe." Tony had all his straps secured and was gathering the courage to sit up on the top of the wall.

"To do the center then, he must have really gobbed inside. Or else peed into it."

"Right." Tony drew in a deep breath and hopped up onto the wall. Jarrod laughed.

"Right my ass. You're not listening."

"Was too."

"What was I talking about?"

"About Lucious's flute. How it caught fire, and he had to pee on it." Jarrod laughed even harder.

"Right. You're not scared."

"Hey, I'm up here."

"Yeah, you're doin' fine. Okay, now for a little flying lesson. Once we take off, the bags really start to make gas. You have to keep releasing it to go down or move around. There's vents on the side. You pull on the right rope to move left, and the left rope to move right. You can also move when you're on your way up, only don't let out as much or you'll stop going up and maybe even go back down. You just have to get a feel for how it works."

Tony nodded that he understood and touched each of the control ropes.

"Okay, I think yours is ready. Now you're gonna go straight up, so be ready to push yourself away from the edge up there. Watch your head. Okay, go ahead and undo your tether, and follow me."

Tony dried his hands on his pants, then pulled the knot out of the tether. Immediately, the gasbag pulled him up off the top of the wall. Just like Jarrod said it would, the bag bumped into the edge of the next layer up, scuffed it, and then started up inside the abyss.

"Watch the top!" Jarrod yelled, moments before Tony's shoulder scraped into the edge. There was about twenty feet between the ground on one turn and the ceiling created by the underside of the next turn up, but it went by too fast for Tony to get ready.

"Ouch!"

"You okay?" Jarrod called out, releasing his own tether. With one graceful swing, the veteran of thousands of flights was able to move clear of the edge and move easily out into the abyss.

"Oh yeah."

"Okay, pull both ropes to slow down." Tony did, and there was a loud hissing noise as gas escaped from his bag. In just a few seconds, his ascent stopped, and his descent began.

"Not that much," Jarrod instructed as the first-timer dropped below him. After a few seconds, Tony stabilized and began to rise again. Jarrod deftly moved in beside him, tweaking the gas release ropes just enough in just the right combination. Their bags gently bumped each other.

“Okay, let’s get away from the side. Wait till you turn a little…now, pull your right side.” Tony did and began to move downward and out toward the middle of the one-hundred-and-fifty-foot-wide hole. Jarrod kept right beside him.

“Doin’ great. Now for the really fun part. Look down.”

“No, I don’t think I can. I might faint.”

“It’s okay. All you’ll do is go up to the top. You can’t fall out. Really.” Tony said a silent prayer, then looked straight down. Seeing his legs and feet dangling above an opening that went so many miles down was enough to push him beyond dizzy. But he held on, struggled to lift his head, and took in several deep breaths. Tropical birds and butterflies scurried to get out of their way as their slow descent continued.

“Good, do it again. Pretty quick, you’ll be used to it.” Even with the birds and the gentle sound of wind, the two could talk normally. Tony followed instructions and was soon used to where he was. Finally, he was even able to smile. He looked over at Jarrod—then let out a whoop of excitement.

“This is amazing! Fantastic! I love it!” The two began to swing a bit, and moved apart so there was more space between them. Pretty soon, Tony was able to maneuver going down and up.

“When you get really good, you can even go completely around. Watch.” Jarrod speeded up his descent and began to swing forcefully from side to side. He yelled out in fun as he went past vertical on the highest point.

“This is it!” On his next swing, he kept on going and went completely over the top of his gasbag. Tony, who had pretty much kept beside him, applauded. “The only problem is… is to stop swinging before you barf….” Jarrod continued to counter his motion, and soon returned to a stable dangling position.

"So?"

"So, maybe next time. I don't want to press my beginner's luck." Suddenly, the entire abyss began to dim.

"Is that me starting to black out?"

"No, it's night coming. This'll be great." Within minutes, the birds and butterflies began to retreat, and the huge fruit bats began to emerge. As the two continued downward, past the screw turns of the never-ending ledge, they were surrounded by more and more of the flapping, chattering creatures.

"Just don't be afraid."

"Why?"

"They'll smell your fear and attack. Tear you to shreds and eat you." Tony was instantly terrified. Then Jarrod began to laugh.

"You jerk!"

"Time for tag!" Jarrod pulled hard on both ropes and began to nearly plummet. Tony held his breath and sped downward after him. Jarrod let up early on his ropes, though, and was already slowing when Tony dropped past.

"Fooled you again." Jarrod pulled again and soon caught up to his friend. Together, underneath mostly deflated bags, they plunged.

"This is like slow sky diving," Tony laughed. After a few minutes in the near darkness, they began to slow.

"We better head back. Watch out." One particularly large bat fluttered right up to Tony's face and came in for a really close look. Then it darted back into the twilight.

"I'm fine. Friendly sucker, huh?" Soon, they stopped, hung there for a few seconds, and started upward again. "What's that?"

"Rain's started. Great." The two fell silent, slowly drifting upward, listening to the sounds of the bats and the gentle pattering of rain drops from between the turns of the ledge.

Twenty minutes later, they reached the top. Tony knew it was the top because Jarrod told him to get ready for a landing. Otherwise, in the near darkness, he wouldn't have known.

A gasbag landing consisted of rising all the way up to the ceiling, bumping it, then releasing gas to maneuver over to one side. Once safely over the ground, all the other gas was released to bring the bag down. Then, before it inflated again, it was dragged back over to the wall, tied to a tree limb, and pushed out over the side.

"That was great," Tony said, breathing hard from the lingering excitement and the exertion of preparing his bag for the next flight. "What now?"

"We'll head out again. But first, I have to do my thing. You can watch if you want." Tony didn't know what it was he was going to watch, so he stayed. The rain continued, and both were completely wet. It wasn't uncomfortable, though, because it was so warm and tropical.

Jarrod stepped a short distance away, removed his handmade clothes, and began to smooth his hands over every inch of his body. It was as though he were taking a shower in slow motion. The process took several minutes, after which he put his wet clothes back on. Billy had come over to Tony to watch too, and gently leaned against his new friend's legs.

"There, that's my version of the Fountain of Youth. Hi, Billy. We had a great flight. Lots of fun." The three started back over to Jarrod's room.

"We'll be going out again, so you be a good little varmint, okay?" Dilly chattered with a bit of sadness but mostly with agreement. Then he stood back to watch as first Tony, then Jarrod, climbed up on top of the six-foot-high, three-foot-wide green crystal cylinder.

Tony helped Jarrod stand. The rain made the top pretty slick, and they had to be careful.

"Ready?" Tony nodded he was, and then the cylinder silently began to rise. In the near darkness, they saw the darker circle of the inside of the elevator shaft approaching. They reached out and let their hands run up the smooth walls as the cylinder beneath them slid inside like a perfectly-fitting plug.

"Now I know what a Navy artillery shell feels like," Tony said.

"Yup. Only we'll end up going a thousand times faster."

CHAPTER FOURTEEN

# Into the Night

A few minutes later, the seemingly magic doorway opened on the side of Tamarra, one hundred and thirty feet up. Tony and Jarrod stepped out onto the large limb, carefully keeping hold of smaller branches. The solid crystalline cylinder silently oozed out of the opening and flowed into the shape of their craft. In less than a minute, it was there beside them, floating on air. The opening in the side of the tree closed.

Jarrod reached over and brushed his hand across the top, and the hatchway lid opened. He climbed in, followed by Tony. The lid closed, and they were ready.

"We're gonna go pretty slow this time, so you can see a little." On that, they were in motion. There was no sound and no feeling of acceleration, just instant motion. The glowing green shell of the craft turned clear, and they were able to look out and around—and especially down.

The moonlit forest streaked by below them. They gained altitude rapidly and could soon see larger features of the terrain.

"This is about three thousand miles per hour," Jarrod guessed. In seconds, they were over Canada.

"Too bad there's not more to see at night." In an instant, anything visible through the bottom of the craft appeared to be in daylight. Tony could only smile.

"Follow that," Jarrod said quickly when something caught his attention. A moment later, they were traveling parallel to a passenger jumbo jet. They stayed beside it for a few seconds, then dropped way down and accelerated away.

"If we wanted, we could have gone in and taken something out of their luggage, the same way I picked up that rock underground."

"What if you went into—or through—someone?"

"They'd feel something, like a puff of almost-solid air press against them." Jarrod looked around. "Now we're probably at six thousand miles an hour." The polar ice flows streaked by below.

"Whoa!" Tony half yelled as they approached a mountainous wall of ice. Effortlessly, the craft rose and skimmed right over the top, then descended again.

"How often do you visit your Fountain of Youth?"

"Every other day. When I started, I only had to do it once a week. Then it was twice. That was about thirty years ago."

"What about every day?" Tony paused in his looking to glance at Jarrod.

"Oh, I won't live forever. I knew that right off. But I don't worry about it." The twelve-year-old pointed out ahead. "Look, there's London." The craft began to slow. "And there's the British Museum."

It was early morning in London. Since it was Sunday, the streets were pretty deserted. The craft stopped, poised above the roof of the museum, then slowly settled through to the inside. They came to rest within and around a typewriter-sized display case. In the middle of the case—now in the inside middle of their craft—was a six-inch diameter shiny black rock, shaped like a very thick bowl. It was still ghostlike, as was its shaped velvet support.

"This is the Shew-Stone. 'Shew' is an old word that means to show, like show something to someone." Jarrod carefully reached out and the object became real in his hands.

He held it so their images reflected from its slightly concave surface.

"It's an obsidian mirror."

"Reminds me of your story-telling thing."

"Yeah. It was made by Aztecs, brought to England after Mexico was conquered, and ended up owned by a guy named Doctor John Dee, who was a scholar and kind of a sorcerer. He said he could look into the black mirror and see the spirits of the dead. At least that's what he told Queen Elizabeth. That was around 1575." Jarrod held it out, and Tony took careful hold. After a few seconds, he replaced it on its ghostlike cushion. Immediately, it too turned ghostlike, seeming to half evaporate into the air.

"Our next stop is just a few hundred miles from here." The craft rose back through the roof, into the early morning light, and accelerated away. In a few seconds, they were above a private mansion near Paris. As before, they hovered for a few seconds, then descended. They were soon in an underground vault, the size of a small bedroom, filled with treasures.

"Now this guy is super-rich. This is what I wanted to show you." The craft nudged over against a locked safe, and penetrated inside. In another locked box, made out of solid titanium, was a fourteen-pound pearl. Everything was ghostlike until Jarrod reached out and grasped his hands around the pearl, at which moment it became fully real.

"This is worth seventy million dollars. It's called the Pearl of Lao-Tzu. It goes back twenty-five hundred years, when a Chinese leader named Lao-Tzu asked that his nephew put a small amulet into a living clam. Carved on this amulet were the faces of Budda, Confucius and himself. He called the other two his good friends.

"What Lao-Tzu wanted was his future generations to wait until a pearl grew around it, then put it into larger and larger clams. It was supposed to be a symbol of peace and cooperation among all people of the world. During the Ming Dynasty, it ended up in the Philippines. A typhoon caused the giant clam to break off its rock and float away, and it was lost. In 1934 it was found again, and then it was sold to a guy in Los Angeles." Jarrod let Tony hold it for a few seconds, then set it down onto his lap.

"This is what's really neat," Jarrod almost whispered. Carefully, he began to smooth his hands across the giant pearl, which was shaped sort of like a big wasp's nest. It started to become ghostlike, but not all the way. Visible inside was the ancient Chinese amulet.

"We're the first people in over two thousand years to see that. It doesn't even show up in X-rays because the pearl is harder than it." A few seconds later, the pearl returned to normal, and Jarrod set it back in place. Then it became ghostlike like everything else around them.

"I hope you like the jungle," the boy said next. They began to move upward and were soon outside again, quickly heading south. In the daylight, Tony didn't dare blink, or else he would miss hundreds of miles of ground below. Cities flashed into rural areas, and then to open ocean, and finally back into night.

"We've caught the night again," Jarrod smiled. "Kind of like playing tag. Ah, we're going to Rondonia. Even though they've stopped burning down the jungle, there're still miners going in everywhere. They're called 'garamperos.' What I want to do is warn this group of natives that they have to go in and get their shots. One of these days, they'll meet the miners and catch the flu or the measles, and then they'll all die."

"So we're just gonna tell them?"

"Yeah. The problem is it's not really safe for us. We can't stay in here or be invisible. We have to talk to them."

"So?"

"So, they might spear us. That's where you come in. I couldn't go on my own because alone, I had no chance. But two is a lot better. If you watch around while I talk, they won't be able to sneak up on us. That's about the only way they do attack, by surprise. If you see anybody creeping around, just make a noise and point over at them, and they'll stop. At least I think they will."

"This sounds scarier than the Root." No sooner than he had finished, the craft settled down in the jungle. They were high up, in a clear area, and could see the horizon. It was just starting to brighten before the new dawn.

"They're just over there. We'll have to make some noise to attract them. You ready?" Tony had no response, and Jarrod stood. The hatch cover opened. The warm smells of the jungle washed in. Birds and insects were starting to move around and make noise.

The two boys climbed down off their craft and stood in the knee-high grass. A hummingbird buzzed past, already searching for its first meal of the day.

Jarrod whispered, "The hummingbirds have these little mites that live in flowers. When one feeds, they crawl up its bill and hide in its feathers until it goes to another flower, then they crawl down. That's how they get around."

"Who cares?" Tony whispered back.

"Oh. Yeah. Sorry. Okay, you ready?" Tony could only shrug his shoulders. Jarrod cupped his hands over his mouth and made a strange whistling sound. A short distance away, more than two dozen natives sprang awake. They were traveling, and so had made no huts. They simply rose out of the grass, from where they had been sleeping, and gathered into a tight group.

"They're the Uru Eu Wau Wau," Jarrod explained calmly.

"You speak…Uru?"

"Been practicing for months. I don't know all of the language, though." One man came forward while the others held back. Tony kept looking around, straining to see into the shadows that were still everywhere.

"I think we should have waited for daylight," he said softly.

"Shhh, I didn't want them to see us that clearly." Then Jarrod began to speak in the native tongue of the Uru Eu Wau Wau. He told the chief he was a messenger from the hereafter, sent by the oldest of his departed sons. Jarrod explained that his son had become a great chief, leader of many spirits, and it was an honor to have been selected to make the great journey to deliver the message. The chief seemed to believe the story.

"Uh oh, there's three coming around behind us," Tony said, trying not to show fear.

"Point, point," Jarrod urged. Tony did, and the men stopped.

"They stopped—but you better hurry…."

Jarrod continued, telling the chief that his son wanted to warn him about a great danger and how the only way to survive the danger was to go to the white settlers' healer and have a magic potion injected under his skin. The chief winced, and Jarrod actually laughed, telling the man that was exactly the way his son had said he would react.

The twelve-year-old finished by telling the chief how grateful he and the other spirits were that he had raised such a great man as a son.

"Okay, wave them away. When they start to move, get back inside—and don't do anything sudden." In the gathering light, Tony could see that each of the three was armed with a long spear. He followed Jarrod's instructions, and the three did start to move away.

"I'm going."

"Right behind you." Jarrod said a few more words, thanking the chief and wishing him much happiness. All of a sudden, the others in the band started to come forward. Even the women had spears.

"What's happening?" Tony asked as he climbed up onto the craft. Jarrod didn't answer, but came up right behind him. Then he slipped—and the natives seemed to jump a few steps closer. With Tony's quick help, Jarrod recovered, and they both made it down inside. Seeming like it took forever, the hatch lid sealed tightly behind them.

"That was too close," Jarrod sighed, a noticeable tremble in his voice. The craft had become clear, and they could see the twenty or so natives coming right up.

"Can they see us?"

"Not anymore, but I think they should feel us, so they think we're real spirits." A moment later, the craft began to move. They went back first, until the three had rejoined the group, then started to move around them. Just like they had done in England, they began to flatten the grass. To the natives, who couldn't see the craft, it appeared the work of an invisible hand.

Suddenly, they were off. The ground dropped away. In less time than it took Tony to blink, he could see the outline of the eastern coast of Brazil. Half the country was in daylight already, and the mighty Amazon River looked like a long black scar on the surface of the land.

Two more blinks, and they were in space. It was amazing to Tony how huge the Earth was—and how beautiful. He had seen many color photographs taken by astronauts, but they were nothing compared to actually being there. Looking down at the advancing line of the new day left him short of breath.

"We're still in slow mode, although not very," Jarrod explained. "This is probably close to a million miles an hour, and we'll be stepping that up just a little."

"I went a hundred once. Pop said he was testing the car, but it was really just for fun." The craft turned, and the entire Earth was visible behind them. The Moon was ahead, coming up fast. In a few seconds, they sped past. The experience was kind of like sitting in a glass chair stuck to the front of a giant movie screen. Only it was not a movie—it was real.

"You know what 'ecopoiesis' is?" Tony shook his head he did not. "It means 'making a new home' in Greek. That's what scientists use when they talk about creating an atmosphere on Mars. You know, spray a little carbon monoxide into the air, sprinkle some charcoal on the polar ice caps, and wait a few hundred years for things to start warming up.

"I think it's a good idea. I mean it's lifeless now, so why not try to make it liveable? Sometimes I think about starting a Root up there. There's still plenty of internal heat to power one, once it gets down deep enough, and it could be just the same as mine. Plus it could even set up something on the side to start making air."

Tony was still pretty speechless. It was enough trying to enjoy the thrill of being in an invisible spaceship hurtling through space at more than a million miles an hour. To try to pay attention to Jarrod was a bit much, but he tried. Then something occurred to him.

"You know what? I wonder if the kids I know feel about me like I do about you."

"I don't understand."

"I like my projects best of all. If we get a new electric motor, like with a neodymium iron boron core, I can't wait to tell the guys about it. But when I do, they look at me like I'm from outer space."

"Now you are," Jarrod laughed. "Just kidding. I know what you mean. Just slow me down if I get going too much on something." What they saw coming up ahead was enough to get even the veteran space traveler excited.

"Mars," Tony gasped. The craft began to slow, and it no longer seemed they would overshoot it by a few million miles. Without a feeling of deceleration, they slowed even further and slipped into a low orbit around the dry and dusty world.

Tony couldn't speak, only gaze out in awe. Jarrod mentally instructed the craft to give them a quick tour of the planet, which included spine-chilling dips into valleys four times deeper than any on Earth. It was as exciting for Tony as life could ever be. Finally, they settled quietly down next to the Viking space probe.

"I just wanted you to see her." The craft moved in closer, and gently merged with the side of the probe. The part that moved inside the craft became ghostlike. Jarrod nodded it was okay, and Tony carefully reached out to touch it. Instantly, the part became real and the craft turned from clear to glowing green crystal. That scared Tony and he pulled back, which caused things to return to as they were before his touch.

Jarrod laughed, "That's our default mode. If something's big and you don't think of how you want it, the Root doesn't know which part you want to turn real, so it does it all. Anyway, let's back up a little and settle—and you can harvest your first Mars rock."

The craft pulled back and settled several inches below the Martian surface. Tony wasn't afraid as the ghostlike soil and rocks rose up around and through them. He reached out, picked up one rock—which instantly became real—and smiled.

"Home, James." Jarrod nodded, and they were off again —this time at full speed.

"This is what I call Warp Speed," was all the pilot had time to say before they were back at the property, alongside the tent. The last cars of a freight train rattled past, and the warm night became still again. The craft submerged itself back into its hole, the hatch opened, and the boys climbed out.

The ship turned green and glowing, which Jarrod left so he wouldn't have to make any lights. He and Tony lifted the tent back into place, spread out some blankets, and settled down.

"Tomorrow, I'll take you on a different adventure. We'll go to the mall." The boy looked at his Mars rock some more, set it down beside himself—and promptly fell asleep, exhausted. Jarrod just smiled, smoothed his hand on his craft to turn it off, and went to sleep too. It had been a day neither would ever forget.

CHAPTER FIFTEEN

# Capture

Jarrod was the first to awaken six hours later. That was about as long as he ever slept in one stretch. It was already daylight, and a train was going by. Without disturbing Tony, he crawled outside the tent and went up to the bush he had been using as a bathroom area.

"That you peein' up there?" a voice called out from the tent.

"I wake you?" Jarrod finished and returned.

"Nah, I was kind of awake anyway. Heard the damn train." Tony crawled out from inside the tent, stood, and stretched in the warm morning sun. "So how you doin'?"

"Good. Last night was fun."

"Yeah, wow. I'll be back in a minute." Tony left for the well-watered bush. "I figure we'll eat at the house then go into town. It's about nine miles. If you want, we'll take my rail bike."

"Sure." Tony returned, and they both started up for the woods.

"I think we can rig an extra seat, or at least a cushion. Oh yeah, nix the Russian clothes. You can wear some of mine."

"Fit in better, you mean?" Tony nodded in the affirmative.

At the house, Victor and Jill were already up, although still in their bathrobes. They were at the kitchen table when the two boys came in the back door.

"Morning," Tony said.

"Morning, men. So how'd it go out in the wilds of East Salem?"

"Same old stuff," Tony answered to his father, wishing he could tell them everything but aware it would sound too unbelievable. The boys helped themselves to milk, toast, and some oranges, and sat down at the table.

"I thought I'd take Jarrod out to Lancaster. Some of the kids will be there."

"Oh, that reminds me," Jill said, "you had a message from Amy on the machine. She says she's going to Portland with her parents today, so she'll call you tomorrow."

"Oh, okay." Tony was quite pleased his almost-girlfriend had called but tried not to show it. Jarrod, who knew all about it from his watching in the Root, took a bite of toast to stop from smiling.

It took the boys about a half hour for Jarrod to change into some normal clothes and to rig a temporary second seat on the rail bicycle. Victor and Jill went through their usual warnings about watching out for trains and then let them go. The trail back to the camp was worn well enough so the tall grass didn't even get stuck in the spokes.

"The only tricky part is getting going," Tony explained as he finished checking the rail with his stethoscope. "All clear." He wrapped up the rubber tubes and folded the instrument into his belt pack. "Okay, ready?" Jarrod was, and the two lifted the relatively heavy bike onto the rail.

"You hold her steady while I get on." As Jarrod held on, Tony mounted the bike. He checked to make sure the tilted-up fiberglass cowling was as far forward as possible. It was, and he said, "Let's go."

Jarrod held the bike steady and ran alongside as Tony started to pedal. Because of its weight, its inertia stabilized it right away.

"Feels pretty steady. Whenever you're ready...." Jarrod began to hop a little with each step, limbering up for the jump onto the temporary rear seat of the moving rail bike.

"Now," the running boy said, executing an agile leap up onto the bike. Tony rolled with the punch, so to speak, and countered most of Jarrod's motion. The bike wobbled severely, and it looked as though they would dump it—but Tony's strong legs pedaled them through.

"Yes, we're going!" Tony yelled. "Okay, watch your head and your hands. Cowling coming down...." The boy pulled on an inside handle, tilting the streamlined envelope down over them. Helped by the oncoming wind, it moved easily and locked into place.

"Hang on!" Only the lower six inches of the extra-wide wheel rims stuck out below the bottom of the sleek cowling. The rest was near aerodynamic perfection. Inside, there was only the faintest sharp whisping of the wind and the fast whirring of the sprocket chain.

"Thirty," Tony called, telling their speed in miles per hour. Already he was straining.

"How's it feel?"

"Not bad. The extra weight doesn't add that ... much." The real struggle began, and then came, "Forty." They were nearly a mile down from where they started, and Tony was just about spent. After a few more seconds of nearly heroic pounding, he gasped, "Fifty-one!" and then let up.

Jarrod let out a whoop of excitement as they began to coast down to a slower speed. It had been the slowest he had traveled in a vehicle in over one hundred and thirty years, yet was the most thrilling. At twenty miles per hour, Tony picked up the pedaling again, at a pace that would keep his legs and lungs intact.

Thirty-five minutes later, they began coasting to a stop. Their target was underneath the Interstate-5 bridge. There were no transients around, just a lot of pigeons, so they felt safe in stopping there. As soon as the oncoming wind was slow enough, they opened the cowling.

"Now the next hardest part," Tony laughed.

"Same way, but reverse?"

"No, you better stay on till we stop. If you shake us up, I won't be able to pedal out of it."

"Okay." Tony gently applied the brakes, and they came to a complete stop. They held steady for less than a half second and started to teeter. In unison, the two extended their legs in the direction of their fall and stopped it.

"Perfect. Okay, you go." Jarrod stepped all the way off, then held the bike steady as Tony dismounted.

"What a team," Jarrod praised. Again in unison, they lifted the bike from the rail and set it down next to a utility pole. A few minutes later, Tony had it secured in place with a heavy chain and lock.

"There're usually some winos here," Tony said. "I used to bring them lunch, but then some different ones came in, and I got scared. They had knives and were pretty mean. So I just keep going if I see them."

"Your folks give a lot to the shelter."

"Oh yeah. We do what we can."

Lancaster Mall was only three blocks from the bridge. The two climbed up the steep embankment to Center Street and walked to the mall. It was almost noon, and already about eighty degrees.

The busses from downtown started running at ten, so most of the kids were already there. It was the only place to be on Sunday afternoon during the summer. Jarrod and Tony were hungry and went straight to Madhouse Pizza. In their usual booth were Darrel Gates, Lance Erwin, and Ernie Botchko.

"Hey, men," Tony said.

"Dude! Where the hell ya been?" Ernie asked.

"Around. Projects. You know."

"Hey, Tony," Lance asked next, "you ever get that freakin' robuttic crab workin'?"

"Robotic," Darrel corrected. "As in robot. Not butt, as in buttocks." He was the too-serious, sometimes stifled one of the group. Most other kids considered him a nerd.

"Oh yes, buttocks," Lance drooled, casting his eye toward some passing fourteen year olds in tight shorts. The others looked too. Then, looking back, he continued, "So, about the crab?"

"It's a spider and, yes, she's working."

"So we'll be over later to check her out." Lance scanned again for passing babes.

"Ah, this is Jarrod. He's visiting." The two slid in as the others made room in the booth. Tony took a sip from Darrel's cup of soda.

"I'm Darrel Gates. Nice to meet you, Jarrod." Darrel extended his hand, and Jarrod shook it.

"Get outta here!" Lance mocked, tossing a piece of pepperoni at Darrel. "Jarrod, huh? That's kind of an unusual name. You know, an old name. A Big Valley name."

"Uh uh, Bonanza," Ernie said. For a few seconds, he and Lance hummed the theme from Bonanza. They tried to get the others to go along, but no one did.

"It's Big Valley," Tony said, standing up. "Want the Special?" Jarrod nodded he did, and Tony got up and went to the counter.

"Where you visiting from?" Ernie asked.

"Gates."

"Ugh, Darrel Town!" Lance gagged.

"That's my last name, like I just said. I'm not from there, though."

"So, ah, what's goin' on?" Lance asked. The bigger, louder, pushy boy made Jarrod a little uneasy. He cleared his throat and shrugged his shoulder.

"Not much, I guess."

"Oh, well..." Lance was mildly poking fun, and mimicked the shrugging of shoulders.

Ernie started, "I was telling them about in England, years ago. My dad's a doctor and has all these great, really gross books about things. They used to make clocks in these factories. There was a whole bunch of people sitting at these long tables, painting the dials with that glow-in-the-dark paint. You know, that green stuff. To keep the point of the brush sharp, they'd go like this, with a little bit of spit on their lips." Ernie demonstrated with his toothpick the way it might have looked.

"No one ever thought anything was wrong. But the reason the stuff glows in the dark is radium. The stuff gives off freakin' radiation! So all of a sudden one day, these guys and these ladies start getting numb parts on their lips and in their ..."

"Like in your head," Lance interrupted, pointing to Darrel.

"In their mouths. You know, I don't know if they were going around drooling or anything like after the dentist, but these parts were numb. But they all just kept working. Then those parts started to turn gray. The tissue was dying ..."

"Necrobiosis," Jarrod added, not even thinking. By the time he caught himself, it was too late. Even Darrel was staring at him. "Sorry."

"Ah, right. So it was dying. And then the parts did die—and they started to rot away."

"Gross. You mean they were still attached?" Lance gagged, letting a piece of pizza hang down from the corner of his mouth. Tony came back to the table then. He opened his hand, showing just a few dollar bills and some change.

"I'll get it," Jarrod volunteered. "I've got a...a twenty. Yeah." He put his right hand into the right front pocket of his borrowed jeans, and began to feel around. Then he breathed in and briefly closed his eyes. Lance leaned in next to him and talked right into his face.

"You got somethin' that big down there you gotta feel around where there's room?"

Jarrod, startled, opened his eyes and recoiled. The larger kid with pizza still hanging out of his mouth gave him a big, open-mouth smile. Jarrod tried to grin a little in response, then finished struggling to withdraw the twenty-dollar bill. The girl behind the counter was getting impatient because she had the register open and other customers to wait on, and was staring too. Finally, Jarrod produced the bill and handed it to Tony.

"Thanks." Tony went to the counter, paid, and came back with two slices of pizza. He gave the change to Jarrod, then returned to get the two cups of soda.

"Anyway," Ernie finally finished as Tony slid into the booth, "they got blood poisoning too and died."

"Sounds tasty," Tony said, raising his slice of pizza as if in a toast, before taking a big chomp out of it.

"My my," Lance observed, checking out more passing girls. "Hey, girls, we have someone here with a king-sized zucchini." He was talking just softly enough not to be heard by anyone else.

"That's real class, Erwin."

It was a struggle for Jarrod to eat, but he did. Then he started to calm down a little. Tony's friends weren't bad, they were just more average types, and he had never interacted with real kids before. What was so unnerving was that his lifetimes of experience and knowledge gave him no special skills to fit in.

Lance finished chunking down his pizza, and said, "Jarrod here taught us a new word: 'Necro-buttic'. It has to do with a robutt with dead lips. You sure his name isn't Alfred?" No one responded, and he just shrugged and sat back with his soda. During the next few minutes, the kids just ate. Darrel was the next to finish.

"School starts in another five weeks."

"Right, Dorko, that's really what we want to think about," Lance scolded, loudly but still in fun.

Ernie laughed, "I know why he's already thinking about it. I mean aside from the fact that he loves the place." In a more quiet voice, leaning right up to Darrel, he continued, "It's the showers." The smallest boy was instantly embarrassed, and looked down. Ernie and Lance laughed.

"Got to face the facts of life of Junior High," Lance instructed. "Gym class with showers. Now, if they were co-ed, then we'd be cooking—especially you, Jarrod my man."

"Uh oh," Darrel said then, after glancing over at the counter. The others looked too. There, talking to the cashier, was one of the mall security men. They were looking over at the five. When the two saw them looking, the girl said something to the man, who took another look at what was in his left hand.

"Jarrod," Tony asked calmly, "was that twenty...okay?"

"I don't know. I was sort of in a hurry. Lance here was ... I don't know. What?"

Lance whispered, "I'm outta here," and nudged Ernie and Darrel out ahead of him. Tony got ready to leave too—and then the security man pointed at them.

"You kids, hold it!"

"Run!" Lance yelled.

"Come on!" Tony said, grabbing hold of Jarrod's arm and tugging him out of the booth. Luckily, Madhouse Pizza was crowded. As the guard started to run toward them, he crashed into some old lady and almost knocked her over like a bowling pin. By the time he caught her, the five had made their escape. Out in the mall, they dispersed in five directions.

"Meet me back at the tracks—and don't run," was all a very confused and frightened Jarrod remembered hearing before Tony lost himself in the crowd. But he was so scared he panicked and did start to run. All he wanted to do was get out of the noisy, people-clogged mall as quickly as he could. Any door or exit would do, but there was none around. Just people and more people. Jarrod ran faster, pushing through all the people. He looked back once to see if anyone was chasing him—then ran straight into another security guard.

"Where's the fire, boy?" the young guard said. His huge hands clamped down around Jarrod's shoulders and almost lifted him off the floor. In a few seconds, the other guard caught up.

"Cops are on their way," the first guard said. Then he looked down at Jarrod and said, "Pretty good counterfeit here, kid, but you forgot Jackson's nose." He began to laugh as he showed the bill to the second guard. "Left off his whole damn nose." By then, a crowd had gathered around.

Jarrod was escorted into the mall security office, where he and his captors were met ten minutes later by two officers from the Salem Police Department. From there, he was brought downtown, to the main police station.

CHAPTER SIXTEEN

# The Adult and Child Services Division

Tony waited back at the tracks for more than an hour, the bike unchained and ready to go. Jarrod, of course, never showed. Then a particularly rough-looking group of transients started to approach from down the tracks, and he had no choice but to leave.

After putting his bike back into the shop, Tony cautiously approached the house. There was no police car there, or even an unmarked detective's car, like Eddie drove. Figuring the police had only phoned, he went inside to face the music.

"Back so soon?" Jill asked. Tony nearly jumped, expecting to be shot on sight. They were in the living room.

"Ah, yeah."

"Lance phoned twice. Is something going on?"

"No, ah, there was just nobody there. That's probably why he's calling."

"Where's Jarrod?"

"Jarrod? Ah, I think he's kind of ... taken off." Tony looked down, and his mother put the newspaper down beside herself on the sofa.

"I'm sorry. So you think he did run away?"

"I don't know." After a pause, Tony finished, "I gotta go." He started down the hallway to his room. His father, coming out of the bathroom, looked serious.

"She tell you? We got a call from Peter Babbage." Victor put his hands on his son's shoulders, and tried to stay calm. "He's the warden at the Oregon State Prison."

"Oh my God!" Tony almost fainted on the spot, thinking he and Jarrod would spend the rest of their lives behind bars.

"He called on a Sunday. A Sunday!"

"Dad, I..." Tony didn't know what to say. Victor let go and stood up tall, and smiled.

"Yesterday, he and Loren Bell were out playing golf. Loren is already so pleased with our Easylink he told Babbage all about it. Babbage thinks that's what they need at the pen to automate their canteen operation, so he called. Guess what? Tomorrow, the Magellans go to prison!"

Tony could manage only a weak smile, and said, "That's great, Pop, really great. Ah... " He looked away and went past him in the hallway, toward his room.

Out in the living room, Victor asked, "What's wrong?"

"I think Jarrod took off."

"That's too bad. He was different, you could tell that right away. I thought he and Tony had a lot in common." The phone rang then, and Victor nearly jumped over to pick it up.

"Victor Magellan. Oh, yes, Lance, he is. Just a minute. Tony?"

"Okay," came the response from the back. Victor waited until his son had answered, and hung up.

Jill commented, "Whatever happened, I think it involved the others. Maybe they picked on Jarrod or something."

"I'm sure we'll eventually hear all about it. Anyway, about tomorrow. You have to dress sort of plain. Don't want to get all those inmates excited and cause a riot. Any of your regular stuff is fine."

"Thanks a bunch!" Jill snapped, taking pretend offense to the remark. Victor sat down next to her on the sofa, right on top of the open newspaper. He was so excited he seemed not to even notice.

"Okay, we'll have to be at our best. Observe and be able to make suggestions, right on the spot."

"We don't know a thing about...what did he call it, the canteen?"

"Right. Actually, we do know. I mean it's a prison. We can suppose. Security is important. We know that. So they wouldn't want things being smuggled in with the cigarettes. How can our system help with something like that?" And so began their afternoon of preparation.

At police headquarters, Jarrod had already been through one round of questioning. He told them his name was Joe Jackson, that his mother beat him up, and that's why he was away from home and couldn't tell them where he lived. He also told them he had found the money, along with a bunch more, beside the railroad tracks, and that he hadn't noticed anything wrong with it.

The detective who talked to him was Hal Driscoll, who was really nice. Jarrod was thankful Tony's uncle was off for the weekend because it gave him more time to escape before the Magellans got involved. They had also fingerprinted him, and called someone from the Adult and Child Services Division. That was the same office Tony and Victor had contact with, but a different group of people.

After all that, they had left Jarrod alone in a room to eat lunch. A bunch of the cops had chipped in and gotten him some take-out from MacDonalds. The boy was nibbling on french-fries, thinking about how to get out.

Escape, Jarrod knew, would have to be all or nothing. He couldn't risk exposing his abilities if he wasn't sure of success. He knew it would be easy to crouch down and make an escape hole appear in the floor, but was not sure where it would get him. He also knew that Tony might be planning to break him out, using the craft but would probably wait until night.

Suddenly, the door opened. In came Hal Driscoll and a woman. She was pretty but had a really hard expression. It was like she never smiled or had any friends.

"Joe, this is Betty Randall from the Adult and Child Services Division."

"Hi, Joe." Jarrod said nothing as the two sat down at the table. "Mmmm, that looks good."

"It's okay. Look, before you start, I thought of something. Why don't you just let me show you where the rest of the money is? I can bring you there and dig it up and then you can let me go."

"That's probably what the FBI will want you to do," Hal said.

"The FBI? Geeze!" Jarrod was getting scared again and tried not to panic. He was terrified of having too many people get interested in him, especially government types. Finally, he was able to continue.

"Okay, so after I dig it up for them, then can I go?"

"I'm afraid it's not that simple," Betty explained. "Unless you tell us where your parents are."

"I can't. I told Hal. I'm in big enough trouble just being late. I don't want to make it worse."

"I can help you, Joe. If there's something wrong in your house, you can tell me."

"There is something wrong and, no, I can't tell you. I'm old enough now to take care of it, and you'll just make it worse. Look, I know you're trying to help. Really. And I think that's great. I do. But this time, you just have to leave things alone."

"What school do you go to, Joe?" The hardness in Betty was starting to show through.

"Uhm...actually, I'm from Kentucky. A little place you probably never heard of. Morris Fork, not too far from Buckhorn. My parents got divorced, and now me and my mom are just out drivin' around looking for work." The twelve year old looked down, trying to pretend to be ashamed. "We're migrants, and we mostly live in the car."

The way Betty's nostrils flared a little when she breathed in made it pretty clear she didn't believe a single word and was starting to get upset.

"Very interesting. Have you ever heard of the National Schoolage Identification Program, Joe? Even Kentucky has it. That's when all school children have their fingerprints taken, in case they ever get lost or kidnapped. That way, when someone nice like me finds them, they can check and find out where they're from. We couldn't find you, Joe. Now don't you think it's time you started telling me and Detective Driscoll the truth?"

"But I am. I didn't go to much school. Lots of kids in Kentucky don't. We're poor. Please, can't I just show you and then you let me go?" Betty stood up, quite angry, and glared down at him.

"No, you can't, Joe—if that even is your real name. Now I don't know quite what, but something here is very wrong, and I'm going to help even if you don't want me to. It's for your own good. At this point, I am placing you into the custody of the Adult and Child Services Division. Detective Driscoll will bring you to our facility at Mounthaven for processing."

"Facility? Processing? No!" Jarrod jumped up, kicking the chair out behind himself, and ran for the door. Hal stopped him, and there was a struggle. "No, no, not me, not me. You don't understand, you don't..." It was no use, and the boy gave up.

"I'm sorry, Joe, but you don't leave me much choice," Hal said before handcuffing him. By then, Jarrod couldn't say anything.

Mounthaven was a juvenile facility, what used to be called a reform school. It was where bad kids were sentenced to, and where all other kids were taken for processing. The ones being processed were not mixed in with the bad ones and were kept in a separate building. As far as Jarrod was concerned, the ride in the back of the police car was a ride toward doom.

Betty Randall didn't even go along. All she did was make a few phone calls and go back to enjoying her Sunday afternoon.

"It won't be that bad," Hal finally said. "We do this all the time. In a few days, you'll be back with your folks, if that's what's best, or else with some temporary folks who will treat you right. It's only hard now."

"My wrists hurt," Jarrod said through the heavy wire screen between the front and back seats of the police car.

"We're almost there. Just a few more minutes."

Jarrod could only sigh out and lean back. It smelled like someone had thrown up back there, and then someone else tried to clean it up. He told himself he had to stay calm and think of a way to escape. It was hard because even with all the windows he was starting to feel really closed in.

It was when he leaned back that Jarrod felt it. The skin on the back of his neck had gotten rough and dry, like that of an old man. A surge of panic rose through him like a wave of fire. He didn't want to, but he screamed out.

Hal screeched the car to a halt, and tried to help. But all he saw was a young boy in a total panic. In an instant decision, he decided the best way to help was to get to Mounthaven as quickly as possible. He radioed ahead, then took off with the lights flashing and sirens blaring. Only the sirens were louder than Jarrod's screams.

A nurse and doctor from Mounthaven were there when they arrived. Hal jumped out and flung the door open while the doctor jumped in. A few seconds after an injection of Sodium Pentothal, the boy became still.

"No, please. You don't understand," Jarrod said groggily. His vision was fuzzy around the edges and he heard a warm hissing sound. "I can't go through this. It makes things happen faster, it makes them faster. It will...kill... me...." And then things went black.

A case like Jarrod's was routine for the staff at Mounthaven. They stripped him, washed him, did a quick medical check, then put blue pajamas on him and strapped him into a small bed in a small room. All the doctor observed was some skin irritation on his back and neck. Every hour they looked in through the window in the locked door to make sure he was okay. In a normal case, a boy like that would sleep for five hours.

At first, Jarrod slept too soundly to dream. The chemical in his blood was too strong for him to be anything but unconscious. Then, as its levels began to drop, the dreaming began. Only they were nightmares.

Back at the Magellan's, Tony was frantic. Ernie, Lance, and Darrel had gotten away clean, but no one had heard from Jarrod. Other kids told about someone being caught and taken away by the police, and it just couldn't have been anyone else. After pacing around for over an hour, Tony had an idea.

In the living room, Jill was saying, "...And I wonder if the inmate clerks actually fill the orders?"

"I'm sure they do. There's only three or four guards there, and they do over a thousand orders a night. They must..." The appearance of Tony caused Victor to pause.

"Hi. Ah, I'd like to go back to Jarrod and camp out again tonight. I probably won't be able to go with you tomorrow. See, what happened was the guys were really rotten to him. He's a great kid, and I'm glad we're friends, but he's ... kind of like me, I guess. He likes all these weird things, and they jumped all over that pretty quick. He didn't really take off from here, he took off from there—the mall. I think I can patch things up."

"I don't have any problem with that," Jill said. Victor nodded agreement. "Why don't you bring some food this time. Jarrod must not have brought that much with him."

"I will. Thanks." Tony started toward the kitchen, then stopped again. "Oh, ah, can you ... sort of leave us alone? Don't stop by or anything?"

"I guess," Victor answered. "Are you sure everything is okay?"

"Oh yeah. Just a lot of stuff happened pretty quick." Tony continued into the kitchen, found a used grocery bag, and began to pack things into it. Jill and Victor trusted him enough to let him go, and got back to their planning for their visit to the prison.

Tony said good-bye when he was finished packing, then left through the back door. He looked back once to be sure no one was watching—then ran as fast as he could for Jarrod's camp. He couldn't explain why, but suddenly each minute seemed very urgent.

At Mounthaven, the real terrors began for Jarrod. He dreamed of being unable to rejuvenate himself because his hands were bound. Rapidly, he began to age. Soon, he died and turned into a skeleton, but was still aware of what was happening. Then, other skeletons came out of the darkness and started toward him. There were hundreds—maybe thousands—of them, all chanting, "We've waited so long, we've waited so long...."

Jarrod's body began to tremble. In the half hour since his last check, he had grown frail and old. His skin wrinkled and dried, his hair turned gray, and all of his body functions deteriorated. For the godlike child, mind was everything that kept him going. Suddenly, his hands began rubbing on the sheet, underneath the thin cotton blanket. The restraints kept them from moving very far, but they could rub back and forth a few inches in each direction.

Gasping, Tony finally made it to camp. He dropped the bag of food and stumbled into the side of the tent, pushing it back a few feet. He leaned on it long enough to catch his breath, then reached down, grabbed under the bottom edge, and lifted with all his strength. The heavy tent came up and over, and rolled over onto its top. Tony pulled the blankets away to expose the top of the craft.

"On!" the twelve-year-old instructed. He hesitated, then rubbed his hand across the closed hatch lid. Instantly, the green crystal came to life and glowed. "Open!" The lid silently rose, pivoting on a seamless hinge. Tony picked up the bag of food, tossed it inside, then got ready to climb inside. Suddenly, the lid stopped opening and the glow began to flicker.

"Oh, no! Not now! Don't go off now! Come on, on, on! Jarrod needs us!" As if the craft—and the Root—heard the words, the glow came back to full strength. The lid opened all the way, and Tony climbed in. Automatically, the lid closed behind him.

"Show me where Jarrod is." A moment later, the image appeared just underneath the inside surface of the craft's shell. "Oh my God," Tony moaned, not believing what he saw. Then his heart skipped a beat. Two little mounds started to rise up underneath Jarrod's blanket, by his hands. The right one rose to a height of eighteen inches. Tiny voices could be heard. They were evil and raspy.

"We've waited so long, we've waited so long ..." The first mound teetered on the edge of the blanket—and then a miniature, moving skeleton fell out off the edge of the bed and shattered down onto the floor. The jaws of the softball-sized skull still moved as the tiny voice continued to speak. As the second mound reached full height, a third one started to rise.

"Go to Jarrod! Go! Go!"

Instantly, the craft was there in the small room. Tony pushed with all his strength to make the hatch lid open more quickly, but it did no good. The second there was enough room, he squeezed up and out and fell down onto the floor. The tiny skull stopped talking and began chomping its jaws—trying to bite him.

Tony kicked it away, stood up, and flung the blanket off of his dying friend. The second skeleton had grown to eighteen inches like the first. It screamed—and attacked. Tony flung out his arm and sent it flying across the room. It shattered into a thousand pieces against the door.

"You'll be okay," Tony cried, unstrapping the wrist restraints. The third skeleton was too underdeveloped to do anything, and just crawled around on the bed, feebly screeching, trying to find something to bite. Tony carefully lifted Jarrod off the bed and brought him to the craft. He was so light it was scary.

Tony climbed in first, then pulled and tugged his friend inside. He tried to be as gentle as he could, so he wouldn't break any bones—but then something snapped. Jarrod groaned out in pain. Tony began to cry.

"Sorry, sorry, buddy. You're almost there. Almost..." All at once, there was a pounding on the outside of the door. One of the medical staff, a great big man, yelled for them to stop, and pounded a few more times. Then he started to work the key in the lock. Tony gave one more tug—and Jarrod came all the way inside the craft. The hatch began to close just as the man came into the room. Tony couldn't think quickly enough and tried not to panic.

"Oh, God, what's that place called? Go ... go to Samarra! Fast!" The man stopped instantly when he saw the shattered bones, screaming skull, and tiny squirming skeleton on the bed. Then, before his eyes, the craft dissolved away into thin air. He cried out and stumbled backwards out of the room. Slowly, the tiny remains from Jarrod's nightmare began to fade away. When the man returned with help a few seconds later, there was nothing there, not even the boy....

CHAPTER SEVENTEEN

# A Long Way From Home

What seemed like only an instant later, the craft settled in Samarra. Tony was too concerned with his friend to notice there were no tree branches visible outside. Then the craft turned from clear to green, and the hatch lid opened.

"Come on, Jarrod, you're safe now. Wake up. Come on, fight. You can do it." Tony gently slapped the withered face, careful not to do harm. Jarrod moved a bit—and groaned again when he shifted his broken leg. Finally, his eyes opened. They were the only part of him that didn't seem terribly aged.

"Here, that's what's hurting you," Tony said, carefully positioning his friend's hands over the broken part. Jarrod nodded slightly, then closed his eyes and began to rub the injury. A few seconds later, he let out a long sigh of relief and opened his eyes. Then—very feebly—he raised his hands to his head and began to gently massage his scalp.

As if by magic, the twelve-year-old Jarrod began to return. He worked on his face next, then his shoulders, arms, chest, stomach, abdomen, and legs. It didn't matter that he still wore the blue pajamas—in fact, it probably helped his hands move more easily over the roughened skin.

Tony wiped the tears off his own face and helped Jarrod sit up against the shell. About a minute later, they both smiled.

"That was too close, dude."

"You know it. Remind me to punch Lance the next time I see him." Jarrod took a few deep breaths and was ready to stand when they heard an unfamiliar noise from outside. He whispered, "Where are we?"

"Samarra."

"You mean Tamarra?"

"Oh geeze, I knew it didn't sound right." Tony followed the lead and whispered. "So where's Samarra?"

"The only one I know of is in central Iraq." There were more noises from outside, and Jarrod brushed his hand on the closest part of the craft. Instantly, it turned invisible.

"Good grief," Tony moaned quietly. They were on the dusty stone floor of a white-brick-walled room, with at least a dozen Iraq Army soldiers pointing rifles at them. The men were instantly puzzled, because they couldn't see the craft anymore, and began to come forward. No one dared to speak.

Then the craft began to blink from clear to glowing green, and finally to unglowing green. The two boys exchanged looks of horror. There rose a frightened murmur from the men outside as they retreated to their former positions.

Tony whispered, "It was starting to blink out when I came to get you."

"It must have waited until we were down and safe."

"Safe?"

"Shhhh. Okay, we have to think fast."

"We could just wait it out. How strong is this thing?"

"The hull is indestructible. The problem is the door's open."

"So close it."

"Can't. It's frozen solid." Tony rolled his eyes, but then Jarrod had an idea and urgently continued, "Here, lean forward. Come on."

"What?"

"Don't argue. Just listen. Forward." Tony did as instructed.

Outside, the post's commanding officer arrived. His eyes widened. In his native tongue, he asked what had happened, and was told it had just appeared in the room a few minutes ago, disappeared for a few moments, and returned. They also told him there were things moving and talking inside.

Commander Rimal ordered his men to stand ready and called out to the craft for its occupants to surrender. The two inside hesitated. Without the Root, they were not able to translate the foreign language. When the order was repeated, though, they guessed what it probably was.

Slowly, in unison, the two stood up so their heads and shoulders appeared above the hatch opening. A gasp rose from the men, and some began to tremble at the knees. Jarrod had transformed both their faces into those of aliens, complete with large bald heads, pointy ears, large eyes, and almost no noses or mouths.

Rimal gestured as he ordered them out. When they hesitated, he drew a pistol from the holster at his side. That was all the convincing they needed, and they raised their hands, which had been changed into long talons. After exchanging looks, Jarrod came out first. Jarrod had also changed Tony's clothes, into blue pajamas. In the short time they had, that seemed the best choice.

Soon, both were down on the dusty stone floor. Commander Rimal said something they couldn't understand, and gestured again which way they were to go. The men nearly fell over each other making a wide opening for the prisoners to pass through.

The moment Jarrod stepped outside into the evening light, he whined out in pretend pain and tried to shield himself. Tony followed his lead. They retreated back into the shelter of the doorway. Some of the men gasped, fearing they were going to be attacked, and one even tripped and fell as he tried to back away. Rimal stopped too, thought for a few moments, and motioned them into the room next to the one they just left.

The two aliens entered the room, and the commander closed the door behind them. Tony wanted to speak, but Jarrod raised his hand to stop him. They went over to the far corner and whispered as quietly as they could, which was difficult because of the strange shape of their mouths.

"I didn't want to get too far from the ship."

"Smart. Now what?"

"We wait. As long as they think we're from outer space, we'll be fine."

"Where is this place?"

"The middle of nowhere. After the Persian Gulf War, they moved their military headquarters here. This is their main weapons storage area."

"Flaming wonderful." Tony touched his mouth, and asked, "You ever see Alien Mine? The Draks." Jarrod's glare made him finish, "Sorry." Then the other boy smiled.

"It's okay. We're gonna be fine. And if we live through this, someday we're gonna laugh about it." They turned when they heard movement outside the door. A few seconds later, it opened. Commander Rimal entered, his gun still drawn. With him, wearing a fancier uniform, was Colonel Amadiya. They stepped aside as several men carried in a small wooden table and four wooden chairs. When the men finished, they backed out, but stayed just outside the open door.

After an almost friendly gesture from the Colonel, the four sat at the table. The boys said nothing as the two men tried various languages.

When Amadiya said, "English?" the two looked at one another. Tony was leaving it entirely up to Jarrod.

"Yes, English." The two Iraqi officers were startled and exchanged their own looks.

"Who are you?" Amadiya asked, having some difficulty with his English.

"We come from far away." Jarrod tried to hiss his words, to give them an authentic alien tone, whatever that might have been. "We come in peace and have no ... desire to destroy your world. You do not need your weapons."

After an almost unnoticeable nod from the higher-ranking officer, Rimal holstered his pistol.

"Why are you here?"

"To visit Earth. It is time we...met." Some words were particularly difficult for Jarrod's too-small mouth to say, especially with the added hiss.

"Do you have great weapons?"

"Great weapons. Weapons so strong a snap of my...a snap would incinerate this entire city." Jarrod moved his right talon as if he might try to make a snapping sound, and both men became frightened.

There was some commotion from outside the room then, and a soldier came in. In his arms was the paper bag from Safeway, stuffed with various American food items. The man nearly smashed them down onto the table.

"American!" the soldier shouted. Colonel Amadiya and Commander Rimal sprang up onto their feet, Rimal redrawing his pistol.

"The truth, please," Amadiya demanded.

"We were ... hungry and stopped for ... food." The men began to speak in Iraqi. Seconds later, two more soldiers came in, carrying sets of prisoner chains. In short order, the two were chained around their wrists and ankles, with a steel ring connecting the chains in the middle.

"Very clever," Amadiya snarled. Then he smiled in contempt at the groceries. "Eat your food. We will deal with you later." The five left, slamming the heavy door closed behind themselves. Outside, the colonel began barking numerous orders. The sound of scurrying boots was everywhere.

"I thought you'd be hungry," Tony offered weakly.

"It's okay. This could get a little sticky."

"How long does the Root usually stay off?"

"A few hours, a few days—it just depends."

Looking around, Tony asked, "Where's the bathroom?"

"You don't have time. We can't stay here. They're nuts. They could do anything." As slowly as he could move so his chains didn't rattle, Jarrod approached the door. He began to smooth his hands near the lock. A few seconds later, a piece of stone appeared, seeming to grow outward from the wall. It stretched and thickened until it securely blocked the door from ever opening inward again.

Through the magic of his touch, Jarrod removed his own chains and then those on Tony. Deliberately, he left the locking bands halfway dissolved, to frighten their captors when they finally broke into the room. Free, the two moved to the far corner, where Jarrod crouched down.

As quickly as he could, the boy began to create. His circular smoothing motions through the layer of dust and sand were quicker than normal, but no less effective. A minute later, a two-foot-wide hole appeared in the stone floor.

"I'll go first," Jarrod said. He scooted around so he was sitting there, his legs inside the hole. Then he pushed off and slid downward. He ended up about twenty feet down, the limit of his creation powers.

"Looks good. Let me go sideways. Then you follow as soon as I get out of the way." Tony squinted down into the dark hole as his companion created again. There was no sound when the new side tunnel appeared. All of a sudden, it was just there. Jarrod crawled up into the new tunnel, and then Tony jumped down into the first one.

Several sideways tunnels later, the two figured they were clear of the building. Jarrod made a chamber next, so they could sit up, and then created some light pebbles so they could see. Finally, the boy changed them back into themselves, figuring there would be no further need for the alien disguises. Both liked the feel of their normal faces.

"Now where?"

"We'll go a little deeper, make a larger chamber, and collapse some of the tunnel behind us." Jarrod rested a bit, and then began to create another side tunnel. Suddenly, something collapsed, and he tumbled downward.

"Jarrod!" Tony called, leaping over.

"I'm okay," came the response. "Be careful, it's a room." Tony held out his light pebble and slid down to where Jarrod had just fallen.

The boys found themselves inside a huge underground storage room. On all sides of them were small crates with red lettering on the sides. It was in some foreign alphabet. When Jarrod picked his light off the floor and held it up, he gasped.

"Semtex."

"What?"

"Plastic explosive. C-4."

"There must be tons of it."

Jarrod thought for a few seconds, then said, "When we leave this fun place, they're gonna remember us. Come on, we better get far away from here." They went to another corner, and Jarrod started another creation routine. As he did, with his eyes still closed, he explained what was about to happen.

"I've got more time for this one. What will happen is another hole will be here, only it'll be wider. But the top part of it will only disappear for a few seconds. So you have to jump down right away, with me. Then it will be gone. Where we are will stay." The boy lapsed into a brief dream, imagining exactly what he wanted to appear. Seconds later, it did.

"Now." Jarrod jumped down, immediately followed by Tony. They looked upward in the light of their glowing pebbles as the opening above simply disappeared. Solid, packed sand returned.

"We don't have to be afraid of a cave-in?"

"Not if I do the digging." Jarrod started smoothing his hands on the side of their hole, and soon there was another cross tunnel. He went first, followed by Tony, who took charge of the small glowing stones.

"So where does all this dirt go?" Jarrod paused from his creating to take a break.

"It gets sent into space, as energy. I don't know where. I think it changes all the time. But somewhere out there, millions, maybe billions of miles away, there's this release of energy. As much as in all these tons of matter. Like millions of hydrogen bombs." There was a pause. It had been many years since Jarrod had asked the same question of the Root and gotten images in the crystal back as an answer. "And all I do is imagine it."

They began to move forward again, averaging about twenty feet every five minutes. Jarrod was actually getting tired. He had never done so much continuous creating before, and his concentration was starting to slip. Finally, he put all of his effort into making a large chamber. It had to be done in several parts, and ended up big enough to park a car inside.

"There," Jarrod sighed, sitting down to rest.

"I forgot. I still have to go to the bathroom." After a few seconds, they both began to laugh. "I'll go back down the tunnel. This should be interesting. Don't go anywhere."

"Need some tissue?"

"Nope, it's not that." Tony approached the sideways tunnel, which was only wide enough to crawl through, and tried to figure out the logistics of what he needed to do.

"There's no way."

"I think you're right." And so Tony just stood there and peed into the opening of the sideways tunnel.

"Better?"

"Oh, much. Wonderful." Tony was tired too, from the pretty strenuous exertion of crawling, and slid down along the curved wall to a sitting position.

"I'll make an air mat and some water in a few minutes," Jarrod finally said, getting his strength back. "Food too, if you want."

"Nah, I'm okay." They both gazed over at the opposite wall, about eight feet away, and tried to relax. It was cool underground, but not too cold. All they had left to do was wait until the Root blinked on again.

CHAPTER EIGHTEEN

# Back to The Root

As they had agreed, Jill and Victor Magellan did not check up on their son and his new friend. Sharply at eight o'clock the following morning, they were at the Oregon State Prison. They were met personally by Warden Babbage.

Getting inside the prison was a slightly scary experience. First, in the main waiting room, they had to walk through a metal detector. Then their pockets and shoes were checked. Finally, they were led down a long walkway to the first sliding metal gate.

After the first gate opened, they stepped inside to the Front Control Room. The gate closed behind them. A guard behind a bulletproof window gave them both temporary identification tags, which they clipped onto their belts. Then a second gate opened, and they went down a long hallway to a third gate.

On the way, they passed the room where new inmates were processed into the prison, and paroled or released ones were made ready to leave. After the second gate closed, the third one opened, and they walked out onto the Control Room Floor.

The Floor, as it was called, was the center of the main prison. The six different cell blocks all connected there. Inmates, wearing blue jeans and blue denim jackets, were everywhere. Some called out greetings to the warden, while others—unseen—called out nasty words. Several also whistled at Jill.

Warden Babbage was popular among the inmates, and never hesitated to pause to say a few words to them. He put off getting into lengthy conversations by advising them to send a kite, which was a prison word for note, to his office. Always, he promised to give it his personal attention.

After going through one more gate, the three stopped at a heavy steel door. One of the canteen guards came to open it and let them inside. There were only two staff members in the canteen that early, Wayne Jackson and Ron Henderson. After the introductions, the three prepared to watch the canteen in action.

The canteen was a large room, right in the heart of the prison, with steel shelves full of most items someone could buy in a regular store. Among the six hundred different ones were potato chips, coffee, toothpaste, ice cream, cookies and crackers, soaps—even Top Ramen noodles and instant breakfast mix.

At fifteen minutes to nine, the eight inmate workers arrived. Each was frisked by either Ron or Wayne. Word spread so quickly inside that they already knew the warden was there with the Magellans. After another quick round of introductions, they were ready for business.

Right at nine o'clock, a guard from the outside unlocked another heavy steel door and let in the first group of shoppers. There were about twenty-five inmates who crowded into the small caged-off area in the front of the canteen. They could not actually come inside and had to pass their order slips through the steel cage mesh.

The order slips were collected and given to Wayne, who looked up each name in that morning's computer printout, yelled out how much money the particular inmate had left, and wrote that amount on the top of the order. Then he passed it to an inmate clerk, who began to walk around with a hand-held shopping basket and collect the various items from the shelves.

Very quickly, things got real noisy. Inmate customers shouted back to the inmate clerks filling the orders, especially when a certain item was out of stock. It was easier to shout to ask if a substitute—and which one—was okay, rather than walk all the way back up to the front.

Once an order was collected, the basket and order slip were given to Ron, who would look at the slip and—from memory—add up the amounts of purchase on a small calculator. There were no price stickers on the items or on the slips. As this was going on, another inmate clerk was putting the items into a grocery bag. Finally, the completed order was slid up to the front window.

By then, Wayne was done with calling out the account amounts, and started handing out the orders. This was done through a sliding steel window. The inmates had to check inside the bag, sign the calculator tape which showed the total of their purchase, and leave. The exit door was controlled by a release button operated by Wayne.

All in all, it was more of a controlled riot than a small store in operation. Inmates frequently complained of being overcharged, and Wayne had only a few seconds to check over the calculator tape and look into the bag. The main cause of the problem was that prices changed every week on some items, but a new price list was only put out once every three months.

For Jill and Victor, it was a feast of creative opportunity. Almost everything was wrong with the operation, and they would have no trouble coming up with many ways of improving it. The three stayed for two more hours. At the end, the two were just as amazed by the confusion as they were at the beginning. When the canteen closed for the first inmate lunch period, the three left.

"Any ideas?" Warden Babbage asked on their way down the hallway, toward the second gate.

"Lots," Jill answered. "With a computerized system, you could tap directly into the inmate accounting records. No big computer printout to keep flipping through. I was thinking of a code system for the items. Like a can of Bugler Tobacco could be a 'B'. The inmates would put that on their order slips."

"Yeah," Victor said, picking up on the idea and continuing it. "You could have inmate clerks actually key in each order, right at the front screen. The system could provide inventory information, so they could discuss any changes or substitutions right there. Then, after an order was all keyed in, it could be totaled automatically and printed in some order."

"Like the order in which the items could be taken off the shelves by a clerk making one walk around the canteen," Jill continued. "One of the benefits I see right off is how quiet it would be. Plus there'd be a lot fewer errors."

"Not to mention keeping the inmates filling orders away from the front," Victor added. "With only a few staff to watch, you know things get pushed through. The inmates keying in the orders would not go to the back where the items are, and the inmates handling the items would not come up past a certain point. All the staff would have to do is watch ..."

"And put a check mark next to each item as he watched the inmate put it into the bag," Jill finished. Warden Babbage was impressed to the point of almost being speechless.

"Do it then. Put together a formal proposal and some kind of demonstration. I'll give you access to the computer people handling the accounts. Ron and Wayne will be able to help too. Very good." They waited as the second gate opened, then stopped in front of the bulletproof window in the Front Control Room.

The warden went back to his office, and Jill and Victor stepped out into the late morning sunshine.

"Feels good to be free, huh?" Jill commented. Victor agreed.

In Iraq, Tony awakened with a start. At first, he seemed confused about where he was. The smell of fresh air, fried bacon, and freshly-baked bread told him he was somewhere else, but his memory and first sights told him where he really was.

"Morning," Jarrod said. "I made us some breakfast. Oh, and there's a latrine down at the end of that little tunnel there. You can even stand up in it—and there's toilet paper."

Tony looked around, still a little groggy, and rubbed his eyes. He tested moving his mouth, which was very dry, and got ready to speak. Before he could, Jarrod offered him a goblet full of orange juice.

"Thanks." After a few sips, Tony realized the heavy goblet was made of solid gold. Then he noticed the plates and utensils, which were also gold. Even the slab of wood which lay on top of the dirt, serving as a table, was ornately carved.

"You okay?"

"Oh yeah. It's just hard sometimes getting used to all this gold."

"When I'd do my magic shows, I'd make about two hundred pounds of gold dust each time. Later on, Dad and I would dump it somewhere. I wonder how many people ever found those piles?" For a few seconds, Jarrod drifted back to the last century.

"It's funny, some things I hardly remember at all. Others, even back to 1865, seem like a few weeks ago." After some more remembering, he finished, "We better eat. Even gold doesn't stay hot forever."

"Excellent," Tony commented. After chewing a little, he continued, "So how we gonna know when it's time to get outta here?"

"The ship will come to us."

"What if they, like, try to dismantle it?"

"They can't. I don't even think they'll try, because they think it's some new American secret weapon. They're probably trying to figure out right now how to turn it on."

"I'm gonna have some big explaining to do to my folks if we don't get back soon."

"Yeah. We'll think of something."

"There's something I was gonna tell you. Not that I didn't trust you or anything. But, well, we sort of tried to check you out. I thought it would be good to know if you really did run away from somewhere—so we could maybe help. You know."

"Yeah."

"So, we ... got your fingerprints ..."

"And zapped me through on the National Schoolage Identification Program..."

"You knew?"

"No, but that's what that lady from the state did. That's okay." Jarrod was actually quite moved that they cared enough about him so soon after meeting to go through that much trouble. And Tony wanted to say that the only reason they went through so much trouble was they had started to like him. But of course neither could say anything because two real men would never discuss mush like that.

"Must be nap time," Jill said as she and Victor pulled into their driveway and spotted Ed's car up near the house, under the shade of a large maple tree. Sure enough, Detective

Edward Magellan was sound asleep behind the wheel. He awakened when he heard them pull up.

"Always nice to see our tax dollars at work," Victor kidded, getting out. Ed got out too, stretched, and came around.

"They take your cop car away?" Jill asked, joining them.

"I wish. It's back in the shop again." Ed paused, thinking of how to begin, then continued, "What does this Jarrod kid look like?"

"Average," Jill answered. "About five feet, dark hair, not too long, brown eyes...why?"

"Sounds like the kid we took in yesterday at the mall for passing a phony twenty-dollar bill."

"You're kidding," Jill said.

"No. But see, the funny thing was it wasn't totally phony. It was misprinted a little, but on the real paper, with the real ink. It even had the serial number of—get this—the last twenty that was printed on Friday in D.C."

"I don't get it," Victor said.

"Hey, I'm just starting." Ed sat back on the trunk of their car, and continued, "Hal Driscoll took the kid to Mounthaven, and he freaked. They doped him up and put him in the ward, and then he disappeared under, shall we say, unusual circumstances."

"How unusual?" Jill wanted to know, getting more concerned by the minute.

"The orderly that says he saw what happened was talking about spaceships and little aliens that looked like human skeletons. They gave him a piss test and he came out clean, but... whatever, the kid is gone. Told us his name was Joe Jackson, as in Shoeless Joe Jackson." Ed paused again, giving them a little time to take it all in.

"Now for the really interesting part. Remember your little fingerprint search?"

"There was nothing," Victor said.

"On Schoolage. But it automatically kicked into FBI, and guess what? When I got there this morning, the match was there. Seems this unknown, small-fingered individual, presumed to be a juvenile, was wanted ... forty years ago as a material witness in a series of homicides in Flint, Michigan.

"There was this cop, now gone, working on these serial killings. Couldn't come up with a thing. Then he got this sort of anonymous letter, written on sheepskin parchment with a quill pen, that told him where to look for evidence and who was doing it. The cop, his name was Clem Caldwell, lifted some prints off the letter and sent them to the Bureau. I talked to his widow this morning. They never found that witness, but they did catch the killer."

"Well that could be some kind of mistake," Jill supposed. Ed smiled, and raised his hand to prepare them for the kicker.

"That parchment letter was signed by someone named Jarrod. No last name, just Jarrod."

After a long silence, Victor took in a deep breath and said, "Well, ah...what do you say when your son brings home a kid from outer space?"

"The son's mother says you two go take a walk and I'll check Tony's room."

On that, they were off. Victor wasn't exactly sure where the boys' camp was but figured it would be fairly easy to find. From the way they talked, he knew the general vicinity. In some ways, Tony's father found the whole situation quite exciting. The boy—or being—who called himself Jarrod seemed genuinely nice. Definitely not a hostile alien. The possibilities were endless.

Close to forty minutes later, the brothers returned to the house. Jill was sitting out on the back porch, with Jarrod's special map and a magnifying glass. It was past noon and getting quite hot.

"Nothing," Victor announced. "Just a flipped over tent, some blankets, and a big hole in the ground."

"And a few solid gold plates," Ed added.

"I think I know where they are." Jill set the magnifying glass onto the framed map, and handed them to her husband. "Up in a treehouse at Opal Creek."

"Good Lord!" was all Victor could say after starting his examination of the amazing object. Ed looked next and was speechless.

Ed finally broke the silence by saying, "My rock-climbing gear's in the trunk."

"Can you stay here? In case they come back?" Jill nodded she could.

"We better hang onto this," Victor said, keeping the map and magnifying glass. "Okay then. Ah, do you think we should do anything? I mean, just kidding around, say we all get captured, and then they come after you."

"No, it's not like that. My instincts are that Jarrod is a good kid—or whatever. I think we're going to have a hell of a summer left. Just be careful. They may not be quite ready to break the news to us."

Jill stood, and the three went around to the front of the house. She and Victor kissed briefly, and then the men got into Ed's car. The detective started the engine, called in on his hand-carried radio that he was being called away on a personal emergency, and drove off. Jill waved once, and then went to sit on the front porch.

Tony's mother was understandably concerned, but excited too. The last time she remembered feeling that way was when there was all the news about the discovery of cold fusion. The advance promised so much help for mankind that she had desperately wanted it to be true. She sat there, hoping again.

CHAPTER NINETEEN

# The Discovery

Not wanting to attract too much attention, Ed decided not to set the flashing blue light on the dashboard. Instead, he just kept moving at about ten to fifteen miles over the speed limit. They passed through Gates less than a half hour later, and reached the Opal Creek turnoff a few minutes after that.

What used to be a narrow wagon trail leading to the Opal Creek Mine had been improved into a narrow gravel road, barely wide enough for a single car. The infinitely-detailed map was so exact, Victor knew exactly where to tell his brother to pull off and park.

"Right up there, over by those bushes. The tree is about a quarter mile that way." They got out, opened the trunk, and took out the rock climbing gear. Although they had removed their jackets and ties, both still had on the rest of their suits— including their dress shoes.

"I didn't think of changing," Victor said, feeling the first pinch on his toes.

The woods were warm and slightly dark. Opal Creek Valley was one of the few remaining stands of old-growth timber in Oregon. The carpet of pine needles, hundreds of years deep, eased the burden on their feet as they moved toward Tamarra.

"There she blows," Ed said quitely, in amazement, when the mammoth Douglas fir came into view.

"Whoa, that's one for the record book." Carefully, the two men approached. At one point, still quite a ways out, they spotted something glinting in the diffused sunlight at about the hundred and thirty foot level.

"That's it, but it's not any treehouse," Ed observed.

"We'll just have to go have a look." They reached the base and set down their gear on the pine needles. Ed quickly sorted and arranged it, and began to snap together all the various pieces and parts. Within minutes, he was ready to climb.

"Here goes nothin'" Ed said, swinging the end of a length of climbing rope around the circumference of the huge tree. It was so big, the end didn't have enough swing to make it all the way, so Victor picked it up and handed it to his brother. One buckle snap later, the jury-rigged climbing strap was ready to test.

Surprisingly, it worked. There was much more stretch in it than the real straps used by telephone linemen, but not too much to make it unsafe. The crampons, which were spiked metal plates attached to the bottoms of their shoes, made it easy for him to work his way up to the first branch. Once he had grabbed hold, he was able to undo the climbing strap. Victor's hands began to sweat just from watching.

There were enough branches after that for Ed to climb up, as if on a huge ladder. Minutes later, he reached his goal.

"What is it?" Victor called up.

"Looks like a glass door. It's stuck at about halfway open. It goes inside. I think you can squeeze in." What neither knew was that the Root automatically formed the opening before it blinked out, to allow Jarrod to return in an emergency. It was open only wide enough to accommodate the boy's size.

Ed secured the rope he had used for a strap to the branch above the one he was standing on, attached a pulley, then threaded it through the end of the climbing rope.

"Okay, come on up. Try to keep leaning out at a pretty good angle, like I did, so you don't slip and fall against it." Reluctantly, Victor began his ascent. With help from above, it was not necessary for him to use their version of a climbing strap. Basically, he walked up the side of the great tree as his brother hoisted him.

Nervous minutes later, the brothers joined. Victor was breathing hard from the exertion—and the fear. He had never liked heights. He held on for his life while his brother secured his safety tether.

"There, you're not going anywhere."

"Tell ... you what. Why don't you go in, and I'll wait this time." Ed leaned inside to look, then straightened back up and smiled.

"Sorry. I don't fit." Carefully, they changed positions on the large, but still fairly narrow limb. Victor could fit in, just barely, and took a deeper look.

"It's all glass. A shaft straight down. It glows a little, kind of greenish." He withdrew and sighed deeply. "Damn I wish you had been the skinny one."

"Okay, look, this'll be a piece of cake. I've got three hundred feet of rope here. If that's not enough, you don't want to go down any deeper." Ed made the necessary connections, then unsnapped the safety tether, then smiled, "All set, little brother?"

Victor rubbed his sweating hands together, rolled up his sleeves, and began to squeeze all the way through the narrow opening. There was no choice but to jump free as soon as he got inside. He did—and the tubular synthetic rope stretched so much that he thought he was falling. He yelled out in fear.

"Whoa, easy, you're okay!" Ed called down, straining on his end of the rope. "How you doin'?"

As soon as Victor steadied himself within the narrow shaft, he answered, "No problem."

"You ready?"

"No."

"Okay, here we go. Nice and easy. Holler if you want me to stop. Sounds like a pretty good echo, so I'll be able to hear you." Ed began to release rope. A special friction device attached to Victor's side of the pulley made it much easier on his hands than doing it all himself.

Slowly, Victor descended down into the faintly-glowing shaft. The first things he heard, other than the pounding of his own heart, were strange chattering sounds. He also smelled the moisture and the humus from the vast tropical forest below.

"Doin' fine. Keep her goin'." The chattering grew louder, and Victor thought he could see a slightly stronger glow from below, where the shaft seemed to end. There was motion too, but he was not sure from what. Suddenly, as he neared the bottom of the shaft, he realized the sounds and motion were from bats—big bats.

"Stop!" The terrified man extended his arms and knees so they pressed against the sides of the shaft, and skidded to a halt. A particularly large bat fluttered up and poked its head into the opening to see what was going on. Victor grunted out in fear, and it dropped away. Before he could call up for his brother to take up the slack, he began to slip. The crystal was just too smooth to get enough friction from.

With a loud yell, Victor plunged fifteen feet down into the large crystal chamber. His rebound on the stretchy rope caused him to start to swing back and forth. Giant fruit bats fluttered all around, curious about the strange sight. The more Victor shooed them away, the further he swung. Soon, he was nearly out over the edge of the abyss.

When he accidentally looked down, he nearly passed out. He was so scared, he didn't even have a voice left. Finally, after figuring the bats weren't going to hurt him, he began to gain control. Realizing there was no way out but down to the floor of the chamber, he called up to his brother

"Keep going! Keep going! Slow!"

Unfortunately, as his brother let down more rope, Victor's swing grew wider. Soon, at his farthest on one side, he was several yards out over the bottomless pit.

"This'll be good..." Victor started to say, just as he saw a brighter glow from down in the abyss. A band of light was rising up from the bottom, passing through successive spirals of the crystal ledge. That was followed by a dark band, then another—wider—band of brightness. The Root was struggling to return to full power.

Outside, what had appeared to be a glass opening began to flicker, as each rapidly-ascending band of light reached the top. With each flicker, the opening started to close.

"Damn!" Ed cursed. "Vic, this baby's closing on me! Vic, you hear me?" The opening was already too small to allow much of the sound inside. Victor heard something, but wasn't sure what. Ed had a quick decision to make. He could hold the rope or let as much out as quickly as there was time left to.

In Iraq, the craft began to flicker with a green glow. An engineer who was inside tried to get out, but the hatch lid closed before he could. The others in the room were not sure what to do and started calling for help. The soldiers in the other room, who had been trying to enlarge the escape tunnel, stopped their work and rushed in.

There was mass confusion. An instant later, the strange ship simply dissolved away, causing the trapped engineer to drop down onto the dusty floor.

Deep underground, half of the craft suddenly materialized inside the chamber where Jarrod and Tony were. They hollered out in delight, and prepared to leave. But then the craft flickered out and became still.

Back at Tamarra, the opening closed all the way, severing the rope. Down below, Victor had just begun his swing in from out over the abyss. He cried out when he felt himself dropping—and landed just over the wall, onto the soft grass. He picked himself up right away and went to watch as the end of the rope dropped out of the opening in the ceiling.

There were more flickers, and then a brief period of continuous brightness. Bats and birds were flapping around everywhere. Above, the opening started to enlarge again, and was soon back to its halfway point.

"Victor!" Ed called out as loudly as he could. Agonizing seconds passed before he heard the faint response.

"Eddie. I'm okay! I'm okay!" Ed was so scared and so relieved he had to squat down to rest and catch his breath.

Below, Victor began to look around. It was twilight again, with just enough residual glow to see. First, he went to the wall to stare down into the abyss. It made him light-headed, and he had to lean there and take deep breaths to return to normal. Then he stepped away and began to look around. The closest opening was to Jarrod's room, and he started over.

The trailing rope caught on something, and he simply tugged it free, without giving it any real thought, and kept on going.

"Hello," the man called in, when he realized it was someone's room. There was no answer, and he stepped inside. He was beside the large bed before he noticed something trembling underneath the ornate comforter. Victor stepped back, and repeated, "Hello."

All of a sudden, there was a terrified shriek as Billy dove out from his hiding place and ran for the opening. Victor let out a startled sound and jumped backward. Then the crystal flickered on again. Victor started to go after Billy, but then decided to look around the room first.

In the chamber behind one clear wall, the bats were fluttering around their roost tree, unsure of whether it was night or day. Only a dark cave was visible behind the other wall. Victor slowly approached it and smoothed his hand on the clear surface, as if testing to see if it was real. Suddenly, the nearly invisible door slid open.

"Hello? Does this mean I'm supposed to go in?" There was no response. "Okay, I'll follow your lead." As Victor started in, some part of the trailing rope snagged again. This time, with more thought, he tugged it free. Then he started to remove the harness.

"Guess I won't need this." The sound of his own voice was quite reassuring, just like he had read in some book years ago. "Wait a minute. If I get lost in there, this might be good for a...trail." Victor left the harness on and started into the cave. Immediately, he crinkled his nose at the pretty foul smell.

The further in the man went, the more he became convinced it was a dead end. There had been a few sounds, which he thought were probably more giant bats, but nothing else.

"Anyone home?" There was still no response. Victor turned and began to walk back toward the opening. Suddenly, behind him, two pairs of huge orange eyes opened. They were moving slowly. Some sense caused him to stop and look back—but the eyes closed an instant before he could have seen them.

"Huh. Must be rats." The eyes opened again as soon as the victim resumed his slow walking. They were gaining rapidly and silently. Victor began to collect the rope, looping it over his left arm.

To the Dark Things, it was going to be a capture too easy to be true. The tiny victim was so slow, so unsuspecting—so oblivious. As they drew nearer, their anticipation grew to the bursting point. Thick globs of venom began to leak from their mouths. Then the smaller one started moving ahead of its larger brother. The larger grew angry and sped up a little too. They brushed—and caused a faint noise, like two soft-skinned balloons bumping each other.

Victor turned and the eyes blinked closed—but not before he caught a glimpse of something. Instantly, he was afraid. He stumbled back and started to run. There was a horrible screech and roar as the dark things began their attack.

The dress shoes with their strapped-on crampons made running difficult. Running fast was impossible. Victor stumbled some more and flung off first his right, and then his left shoe. By then, the beasts were almost on top of him. He cried out and continued to flee.

One mighty claw slashed outward, its scythelike hook gashing down across the man's back. The dark object was so sharp, it didn't even slow Victor down as it opened his shirt and severed two of the harness straps.

Victor plunged through the opening, through Jarrod's bedroom, and out onto the terrace. The Dark Things screamed when they reached the opening. It was too small for them to get through, and there was a brief struggle over which one would go first. The Root had blinked off again, and so the door remained open. After much squealing and slashing, the larger beast squeezed through. Seconds later, the smaller one followed.

The terrified man slammed into the four-foot-high wall, almost toppling over into the abyss. There was another screech, as the larger Dark Thing made its killing lunge. There was no choice, and Victor hurled himself over the edge.

It was too late for the monster to stop. With a scream more evil than anything that had ever been heard on Earth, it tumbled over the wall and into the abyss. The smaller beast, a few seconds behind, had time to skid to a stop. Great chunks of grass and soil plowed up in front of it.

In one fast swoop, the stopped dark thing had the rope in its claw. It was difficult for it to grasp around something so small, but it squeezed and squeezed until the sliding stopped. Nearly two hundred feet below, Victor's freefall ended and the rope began to stretch. He yelled as it bottomed out, struggling to hold himself inside the damaged harness. Then his rebound began, hurtling him in toward the side of the abyss.

Victor slammed into the top of a large tree just as the larger beast hurtled past. The scream was something he would never forget. Immediately, he started to climb inward—but then the rope tugged violently and he was pulled outward. The Dark Thing was reeling him in!

"No way!" the man yelled, struggling to work free of his harness. As he scraped up through the next tree, he unsnapped the last hook and fell loose onto the branches. They started to give way and it seemed like he might fall all the way through, but he finally managed to grab hold. Gasping for air, he clawed his way closer to the safety of the ledge.

Just as Victor made it, he heard the terrible roar from the monster above. He knew it would come after him. All at once, the intermittent brightness came up to full intensity. There was no more flickering. The man crawled over the wall and fell onto the soft ground, too exhausted to care.

CHAPTER TWENTY

# The Rescue

Deep under the ground of Samarra, Iraq, the craft began to glow steadily. The boys cheered and shook hands.

"Come on, we've got some clean-up to do." Jarrod stepped up on the side of the craft, ready to climb in.

"Wait a minute. What about all this stuff?"

"Just leave it. We can make more if we ever need it." The twelve-year-old entered his craft. It pained Tony to walk away from tens of thousands of dollars worth of pure gold, but he finally did. After he climbed in, the hatch lid closed over them.

"Okay, now we kick some butt." On instructions from his thoughts, the craft dematerialized and appeared an instant later in the chamber full of plastic explosive. They stopped halfway inside of a case of the Semtex. Jarrod smiled and withdrew a small, marble-sized cube of crystal from the pocket in his pajama tops. As soon as he set it down, it turned ghostlike like the other contents of the case.

"Just a little something I whipped up with breakfast. Show me their other stockpiles." An image appeared just inside the surface of the craft's hull, like a three-dimensional map. It showed them what was happening in real time, including all the people moving around. Jarrod pointed to the different areas in turn and said, "Take me there, there, and here."

Less than a blink later, they were inside of the first location the boy pointed to. Jarrod set another charge. They repeated the process twice more.

"I don't see how leaving them with all this stuff qualified us as having won the war."

"I don't know. Maybe it was a great political victory."

"Right," Jarrod answered sarcastically. "Okay, take us up for the message." Slowly, the craft began to ascend, up through the fifty feet of packed sand and concrete above the weapons bunker.

The craft emerged into the night a few inches from a group of men. At first, none was even aware of it. As it continued to rise, it began to materialize. The first shout came, followed by many shouts. Terrified soldiers scurried everywhere. The craft turned almost clear, making it appear to those on the ground like Jarrod and Tony were suspended twenty feet in the air.

Colonel Amadiya and Commander Rimal stumbled out onto the second-story balcony of their sleeping quarters. Neither was in uniform. Searchlights were turned to point at the two in the nearly invisible ship. They both smiled and waved.

"This is what I'll call my Superman Speech," Jarrod started. "You know, *Truth, justice,* and all that. Okay, translate and broadcast. Greetings..." The boy paused to look around at all the rifles and machine guns being pointed in their direction. He was about to continue when Tony leaned over and whispered something into his ear.

"You sure we're not going to blink out again?"

"I hope not," Jarrod whispered. Then he continued, "You were right, Colonel, we are Americans. And damn proud of it. You have ten minutes to evacuate. We have decided to destroy your weapons and explosives. You may thank your Allah that we are a kinder people than you and have decided not to destroy you. If you do not settle in peace, Colonel Amadiya, we will be back. This will be your last warning."

Commander Rimal pulled a pistol out from behind his back and began to fire. All the soldiers followed. The night erupted in a barrage of bullets. Those that struck the craft recoiled harmlessly, trailing great sparks.

Inside the craft, it was completely silent. Tony was quite uneasy, but Jarrod remained calm. "You have wasted two minutes. You have eight minutes left." Within a few seconds, the number of bullets striking the outside diminished. Some soldiers threw down their weapons and began to run. Others fired until they were out of ammunition, and then ran.

The Colonel began to yell at his men, but no one listened. Even Rimal was getting scared. Finally, Rimal fled back into the room. Amadiya stayed the longest, shouting unheard insults at them, but then decided to flee, too.

The craft pulled up and away, and was soon out of range of the last soldiers who were shooting. It stopped about a mile away, so Jarrod and Tony could watch. Like ants abandoning a nest to a flood, streams of terrified soldiers fled the military base. Jeeps and trucks, packed full, moved out, too.

"You think they'll all get out?"

"The charges won't detonate until the last man is at least a quarter mile away. From the looks of it, that won't take very long."

"Were there chemicals?"

"Oh yeah. But we're not exploding them. They're deep enough where the other explosions will just bury them. I didn't want to take a chance on a release."

Soon, what appeared to be the last man straggled out after all the others. The two watched tensely, their excitement growing. No one followed.

"I think that's the one," Tony nearly chirped. "Okay, say when you think he's at a quarter mile." They both held their breath for what seemed like a long time. The ant-sized figure continued to move away from the compound.

"I think now ... " Tony started. Before he could finish, there was an incredible flash of light. "I want to hear!" Jarrod nodded, and suddenly they could hear.

The entire compound seemed to rise into the air, as if being pushed upward by a gigantic mushroom. Entire buildings shot up like odd-looking rockets. An entire mountain of dust and other flaming debris followed.

The shock wave, looking like a rapidly-expanding bubble, moved outward faster than the debris. The boys held their ears as it approached. In a flash, it was past them. The loudest thunder they had ever heard slammed into them, causing them to recoil. It lasted only a second, then lowered to a less intense roar. Finally, it became a loud rumble.

Jarrod and Tony cheered as the enormous quantity of debris began to settle.

"That'll take hours. Well, partner, what do you say we head home?"

"Sure. But go kinda slow. I need to think of an explanation for my dad." Jarrod smiled, and they were off, cruising at only tens of thousands of miles per hour. The land below began to streak by. Soon, they caught up to and crossed the line between night and day. After only a few minutes more, they began to slow over Oregon.

"Uh oh," Jarrod said, pointing ahead. "There's someone at the tree."

"Just go to camp then." Tony hadn't seen yet.

"I mean up in the tree. Look!" Tony did—and almost fell back.

"That's Eddie! My uncle, the one I told you about."

"Geeze!"

"Wait. It might not be that bad. He might have just found our map. He might not have seen anything. Can you get in close?" They did—to within a few dozen yards. The man looked over, sensing something, but could not see them. He was just sitting there, looking quite dejected.

"Something's wrong. Appear, go ahead, appear!"

The craft moved in and began to materialize. The hatch lid also opened, and Tony stood up to look out. Ed was startled, but not enough to lose his balance.

"What's wrong?" Tony asked.

"Victor's down inside. There was an opening. It went back and forth, and then it closed." Ed paused when Jarrod appeared, then finished, "But then you two probably know that already."

"Ah, this is Jarrod. Jarrod Blackwell."

"Alias Joe Jackson?"

Jarrod nodded a bit, acknowledging the fact, and said, "Hi, Ed." He climbed out onto the branch, and Tony followed.

"How much rope did he have?"

"About two hundred feet, Jarrod. Then the thing pinched it off."

"He's fine then. It's not that far to the bottom."

"If that's the bottom he ended up on," Tony said, growing more and more concerned.

"Hang on, we'll go down and look." All of a sudden, the craft began to flicker.

"Oh no, not again. Hurry!"

"Just stay calm." Jarrod thought for a second. The craft moved forward and made gentle contact with the tree. The opening appeared, and it started to flow inside.

"It would take too long to explain," Jarrod said even before Ed could ask the first question. "Just do what we tell you, and we'll all be fine. Come on, you climb in there, feet first. Tony, you go next. I'll ride down on your shoulders."

The flickering got worse, but everything kept working. Ed did exactly as instructed, and the boys followed. Soon, they were on their way down to the Root.

"Hold steady and I'll try not to lose my balance," Jarrod said as they cleared the bottom of the shaft.

"Whoa!" Ed called out, waving his arms to keep steady. In the process, he almost knocked Tony off, but caught him. As soon as the crystalline cylinder touched down on the floor, the entire place dimmed.

"Pop?" Tony yelled. "Pop? Where are you?"

"Victor?" Ed's voice was much stronger.

All of a sudden, Billy came scampering out from hiding and ran to hug his master.

"Hi, Billy." The small creature began to cry and fret, and would not calm down. He began tugging at Jarrod, trying to get him to go toward his room. Just as Ed spotted the remains of the harness and what was left of the rope, over near the wall, Jarrod slowly sank to his knees. It was as if someone had let the air out of his body.

Billy became so scared he fell silent, and took a few steps back. Tony noticed, and looked down at his friend.

"I found this," Ed said, bringing the shredded harness back with him. Tony motioned for him to be quiet.

"What is it, Jarrod?"

"A Dark Thing is loose. Can't you feel it?" Neither could, and the boy looked at the harness in Ed's hand.

"What about my dad?"

"I don't know. I think he's okay. It's ... still hungry. It wouldn't be hungry if it had ..."

Ed went over to the wall and looked down into the abyss. Even in the very faint light, the sight was overwhelming. Like the others before him, it took a few seconds for him to steady himself.

"Victor?" he called down. "Victor?" The noise from the bats was pretty loud, but the sound traveled. Jarrod jumped to his feet when the reply came.

"Ed? I'm down here." The three strained to look downward. It was too faint to see more than a few dozens turns down, and Victor's voice was coming from just beyond.

"Are you okay?"

"I can't move real well. But...listen, there's something after me. It might be after you, too." Ed turned to the boys.

Jarrod said, "Tell him we know, and to start moving downhill."

"Victor, the boys are with me. Jarrod says he knows and to start moving downhill. You got that?"

"I'll try. One of them is dead. It fell over into the hole." Ed looked back at the boys, but the news didn't seem to matter much to Jarrod.

"I'll go now. Be careful."

"Can't you make us a gun or something?" Tony asked.

It was as if Jarrod could only half hear what was being said. Even in the dim light, the other two could see he was almost in a trance. Slowly, he shook his head that he could not. His voice was weak.

"It's too strong. To make something, I have to concentrate. All I can think about is it." Something frightened him then, and he gasped. Tears welled up in his eyes as he looked at the others. "It's feeding now, getting stronger. It...it's trying to make a body for itself. It wants to stay in this world."

Without warning, they heard a loud growl from somewhere on the other side of the abyss. There were some crashing and tearing sounds too.

"It knows we're here," Jarrod said quietly.

What they couldn't see would have made them even more scared. The dark thing was moving through the jungle, grabbing any living thing it could reach with its claws. It had already devoured dozens of birds and bats, and had enough material to start forming a skeleton. Visible inside the towering dark form were nearly half of its massive leg bones.

"Do you have a gun?" Jarrod asked next. Ed reached down and pulled a .44-caliber, Colt semi-automatic out from its holster underneath his shirt.

"Twelve rounds. Extra clip's in my jacket in the car. You think this thing can be shot?"

"I don't know. If it's starting to be real, we should be able to damage it. If anything can damage it, that can."

"I better go alone. I'm sure I don't need to ask what to look for."

"No, too dangerous. It's too smart. You'd never see it, and you wouldn't have a chance. No, we've got to bring it to us." Jarrod's voice quivered with fear. He took in a deep breath and continued, "I have an idea. I think we can surprise it enough to give you a chance to shoot it."

"I'm ready."

Jarrod looked around, then shrugged his shoulders as if realizing there was no good place to do what he had in mind. He crouched down.

"Tony, you and Billy go down there. If this doesn't work, just keep on going. Catch up to your dad, and all three of you keep on going. You can go down almost forever. The

Root will come back on by then. Ask it for help. It should understand you. Go." Tony grabbed Billy and retreated.

"You stand there. When you see it, shoot. Don't worry about me." Ed stepped a few yards away and assumed a target-shooting stance, with both hands ready on his weapon.

Jarrod cleared a small area of soil and began to smooth his hands. Since all he could concentrate on was the monster, that's exactly what he did. He let the horror and the fear flow in, turning his dream of creation into a nightmare. The boy held his breath and watched for the distant speck of light—then imagined with all his power that the beast was right there with him.

An evil howl pierced outward from the darkness of the abyss as the monster was startled. It roared next, trying to cling to its existence. But it was not strong enough, and was pulled away into the void.

Moments later, a mound began to rise up underneath Jarrod. It grew faster and bigger than even his worst fears could have prepared him for. He wanted to scream but continued to create. More and more of the evil form gathered below him, pushing him higher and higher. It was all around him too, as though he were on the roof of a buried car.

Jarrod reached down and screamed. His hand had touched something hot and slippery. All at once, a massive claw emerged from the soil, hurling him a dozen yards away. He crashed to the ground, briefly stunned.

Ed yelled too, but held his fire. There was still no clear target. Then the beast erupted from the ground, as angry as all of hell. It bellowed out and clambered to right itself, its massive claws gouging huge chunks from the ground.

The gun began to fire, all twelve rounds slamming in around the head and eyes. Every shot was a perfect one. The monster screamed again and tumbled backward, but quickly recovered. It was hurt, great oozes of black, tarry goo appearing between and in its eyes— but it was still alive. It was unsteady too, but able to start for them.

"Let's go," Ed yelled, darting down to fetch Jarrod and catch up to Tony and Billy. He had already started to reach, but the boy looked up and shook his head not to disturb him. Ed tried to change the direction of his momentum and crashed down to the side.

Ed picked himself up and retreated, knowing not to disturb Jarrod, who was creating again. The boy stood his ground, slowly and carefully smoothing his hands through the rich forest soil. The monster loomed above him but he did not waiver. Surprisingly, the wounded beast paused. Why the puny little human did not flee confused it for a few seconds.

They were the critical few seconds Jarrod needed. Gathering all the strength he had, he looked straight up at the oozing eyes of the monster. As he did, a smaller mound began to grow beneath his hands.

"I created you, and I have the power to destroy you. You're nothing. I have the power." A low rumble started deep in the throat of the beast, building up to a bellow. Its mighty claws began to open and close, sounding like massive, rough-edged scissors.

"My power is strong enough to create you all over again, any way I want. This is how I want." Jarrod stood, pulling from the ground a living, screaming, writhing replica of the larger beast. "By my power, you and this are one. Whatever I do to this shall be done to you. I made you both, and it's as I say."

The larger beast lunged, trying for a quick severing of the boy's head—but Jarrod moved even more quickly, plucking off an arm of the replica. The larger one screamed as its arm pulled off and dropped to the ground. It tried with the other claw, but Jarrod beat it again, tearing off its second arm.

"Go back now to the hell from which you came, and never come again." The armless monster screamed, the replica screeched—and Jarrod gave a massive tug that pulled the body of the smaller one apart. It was as if the larger exploded in the middle, sending a shower of foul-smelling globs in all directions. The boy dropped the pieces from his own hands, and the larger ones toppled over too.

Jarrod looked around, surprised to hear nothing. It was the first time since its creation that the Root was silent. All the bats and other living things had fled away from the evil. Then, the first bat fluttered back, followed by more.

Tony, Billy, and Ed emerged from the twilight. Billy and Jarrod hugged—and then so did Tony and Jarrod. All four looked up in happiness as the green glow flickered back on. It came on strong that time—and stayed on.

"You okay up there?" Victor called then. Tony ran to the wall and yelled down.

"We're okay!"

"That was some racket, even from down here. Is it safe to come up?"

"It's safe! We're coming down!"

"Just don't do it the way I did!" Tony began to laugh, and stepped back to join the others.

"Come on. We got some pretty fancy explaining to do, partner."

"And we're even alive to do it." Jarrod wasn't sure whether to laugh or cry, so he did neither. All he knew was he had not been as happy in a very long time.

THE END